John Creasey – Master Storytell

Born in Surrey, England in 1908 into a poor family in which there were nine children, John Creasey grew up to be a true master story teller and international sensation. Writing under multiple pseudonyms, his more than 600 crime, mystery and thriller titles have now sold 80 million copies in 25 languages. These include many popular series such as *Gideon of Scotland Yard, The Toff, Dr Palfrey and The Baron.*

Never one to sit still, Creasey had a strong social conscience, and stood for Parliament several times, along with founding the One Party Alliance which promoted the idea of government by a coalition of the best minds from across the political spectrum..

He also founded the Crime Writers' Association, which to this day celebrates outstanding crime writing. The Mystery Writers of America bestowed upon him the Edgar Award for best novel and then in 1969 the ultimate Grand Master Award. John Creasey's stories are as compelling today as ever.

Good & Justice

(Gideon's Drive)

John Creasey

(writing as JJ Marric)

HOUSE OF
STRATUS

This edition published in 2013 by House of Stratus, an imprint of Stratus Books Ltd., Lisandra House, Fore Street, Looe, Cornwall, PL13 1AD, U.K.

www.houseofstratus.com

Typeset by House of Stratus.

A catalogue record for this book is available from the British Library and the Library of Congress.

ISBN 07551 - 2344- 1
EAN 978 - 07551 -2344-5

MOOD

I HOPE he won't be late tonight, Kate Gideon thought; tonight of all nights. The words went through her mind as she stood in front of a tall dressing-table mirror, the centre one of triple mirrors in a burr-walnut suite darkened only slightly with the twenty-five years it had been in this room: hers and George's. She tipped the mirror so that she could see herself in a straight reflection; and then moved the side mirrors so that she could the better see her left and right profile.

As objectively as a woman could, she studied the result.

On the whole, she was content with it.

She was used to her looks and it did not greatly concern her that she was a handsome woman, as indeed she was, with dark hair showing remarkably little grey for a woman in her early fifties. It was good when George, or any one of the children, for that matter, told her she had lovely grey eyes, but she was no longer flattered by such compliments: or at least, very seldom. She looked now for the added or the deepening lines at her eyes, the corners of her lips, her forehead; and she really did not think she had acquired more – at least not many more! – since she had last allowed herself time to dress and make up so as to go out with her husband.

It was twenty minutes to seven on a pleasant August evening;

he was to be here at a quarter to, so he was not yet late. They were going to dine out for a variety of special anniversaries: one for their wedding, weeks past now; one for his birthday which had been at least two months ago. One, the anniversary of the day when they had moved into the solidly-built house in Fulham, a residential part near the Hurlingham Polo grounds and tennis courts. Then, it had been much as now; the red brick had mellowed and toned down slightly, like all the others in this terrace of houses, forty-four on this side of the street each with a solid wall dividing it from its neighbour on either side. Grey slate roofs, painted woodwork mostly black and white or green and white; coloured glass panels in each front door, tiles in vari-coloured patterns on the porch and on the path leading from the iron gate which led from the street itself.

Neither large nor luxurious, but highly respectable and worth, today, ten times the fifteen hundred pounds Gideon had paid for it; it was a kind of symbol of Gideon himself.

She went to the sash cord windows in the small bay, and looked out. The cars of their neighbours were parked nearby. A few couples were already going out. The homeward rush was over, then, but George—

The clock in the dining-room struck the quarter to, melodiously in a homely imitation of Big Ben. *Da-da-da-dahhh, da-da-da-dahhh, da-da-da-dahhh*, the last note echoing faintly. She watched traffic passing the end of Harrington Street, thinking: "He *is* late."

Then she laughed at herself and told the big room: "*Minutes* don't count."

But as she knew well, minutes often counted very much indeed in the life of a senior officer of London's Metropolitan Police, the Commander of the Criminal Investigation Department and a man who had won the distinction, over more years than they had been married, of becoming the most renowned and dependable policeman in all England. George himself was probably the only one on the Force who did not believe this; unless, of course, he took it for granted.

But it was unlikely that he thought about it at all, merely going on with his job, as he always had. Whatever the cost, to him or to her, he had been a policeman first, husband, lover and father afterwards.

She caught her breath.

There was an unexpected whiff of criticism in this reflection, and it pulled her up short, made her ask herself whether it was really true. She repeated the words in a whisper which came back to her gently from the shadowed room.

"A policeman first, husband, lover and father afterwards."

Why on earth should such a thought enter her head now? Because he was two or three minutes late for an evening date which was probably of much greater importance to her than to him? Of course if she really thought that, thought he was taking her out simply to please or to humour her, then she could understand the unexpected trend of her thoughts: unexpected because they had come so suddenly and no vestige of them had shadowed her getting ready for the evening.

Once he was here, they would vanish.

"No," she said aloud to herself, "they won't vanish. They'll fade into the background and stay there painlessly for weeks, perhaps for months."

Painlessly?

If he were seriously delayed, if he had to call and tell her the evening was off, or seriously late, it would hurt, whether there was justification in that or not. For some reason she simply did not understand, she was feeling more strongly about – against – the lot of a policeman's wife than she had for a long time, certainly for years. When she made herself think back she remembered that in the past few months he had been forced to call off an evening out, or a much-anticipated family evening at home, more often than she could recall since he had been promoted from Chief Detective Superintendent George Gideon to Commander of the Criminal Investigation Department, the highest step he could go; or as high as he was ever likely to allow himself to go.

3

She looked out of the window again, saw no sign of him, and went back to the dressing-table. She gave a perfunctory look at herself in the mirror, and another as she picked up pale, biscuit-coloured gloves of thinnest leather and a matching handbag. She wore a russet brown suit, not quite right for her grey eyes and colouring, but fitting perfectly; Junoesque, they had called her at school, and Junoesque she was still. If the reflections pleased her, her mood did not, and it was the mood which had the upper hand again when she reached the foot of the stairs.

George must be ten or fifteen minutes late.

The stairs, behind her, were steep, carpeted from wall to banisters, like the landing above the four bedrooms, of which only theirs was now occupied. That could have something to do with how she was feeling, of course: loneliness. Penelope, their youngest daughter, was touring Australia with a BBC Symphony Orchestra and would be away for several weeks, returning to be married almost at once. Malcolm, their youngest son, was also away, touring Europe with a group of youths about his own age. When he came back he was going to ask them if they minded if he shared a flat with one or two friends; and they, she and George, would have to say that of course they didn't mind, that he must live his own life. The old, trite truisms; true, certainly, but leaving the emptiness of the heart hollow and hurting.

Why was her mind so full of the thought of hurt tonight?

Was it because she had literally nothing to do, no one to prepare for? She walked listlessly through the living-room, into the bright, recently refurbished kitchen which had a window overlooking the long garden. The light was good enough for her to see the formal grass on one side, the crazy-paving she and the boys had laid, and an herbaceous border bright with flowers. Everything was spick and span out there, even the vegetable patch beyond lawn and flowers, divided by a box hedge, over which could be seen the scarlet blossom of runner beans.

The big refrigerator hummed.

The kitchen glistened and glowed.

"I haven't enough to do!" Kate Gideon exclaimed suddenly.

A car door slammed outside.

"There he is!" she exclaimed, and in spite of herself her heart leapt, she snatched another glance in a mirror on the passage wall, saw George's shadow approaching the coloured glass panels of the front door, and then with a clang of disappointment, realised that it wasn't George; whoever approached was too small.

He—wasn't—coming.

She steeled herself to show no expression except a superficial pleasantness as, almost simultaneously with the ringing of the bell, she opened the door. In the porch, backing away in anticipation of her approach, was a rather short, elderly man whom she knew well by sight, and who had often driven her and Gideon. A messenger. He had a lined and leathery face and deep-set blue eyes which kindled at sight of her, no doubt at all in admiration.

"Good-evening, Mrs. Gideon."

"Hallo, Mr. Ferris."

"The Commander's very sorry"—she had to school herself not to show her disappointment—"but he got delayed at the last minute, and won't have time to come home and then get to the restaurant in time. So he sent me for you, and he'll meet you there."

"Oh," she said, and gave a little breathless laugh before confessing. "I thought for a moment he—" She didn't finish, but turned into the hall. "Come in – I won't be two or three minutes."

"I'll wait in the car," said Ferris, "if that's all the same with you. Better not stay double-parked for long even outside the Commander's house. These young coppers today, no respect for their elders!"

He turned away, smiling; and she carried a picture of a humorous mouth and twinkling eyes. She went into the front room, which was the biggest in the house except for their bedroom immediately above it, and stood there for a few seconds, quite absurdly affected and full of self-reproach. Why *had* she felt so?

Did it matter, now that she was on top of the world?

She went out only a minute or two after Ferris, who was standing by his big, old-fashioned car, one used to carry the Yard's VIPs to appointments. Across the road she saw a small red sports car with the word 'Doctor' on the windscreen: and it made her pause. This was a new doctor in the neighbourhood, Kelworthy, already making himself popular as one of the 'old sort', which meant that he made house calls promptly and spared time to talk with his patients.

Why was he there this evening?

She knew that the young girl who lived in a flat in the house almost opposite was within days of having her first child; it wouldn't have surprised her to see a taxi; or the girl and her husband going off in a neighbour's car, for they had none of their own. But the doctor—

"Is there something the matter?" asked Ferris.

"Yes," she said, "but I'm not sure what. You can wait a few moments, can't you?" Without waiting for him to say yes or no she walked across the smooth surface of the road, with a grace which Ferris, who had always had a soft spot for the Commander's wife, watched appreciatively.

The house was owned by a Mrs. Jameson, whose husband had died leaving her very little to live on; with the help of relatives she had made three flats in the house, ground, top floor and attic, and lived mostly on the rents. She was older than Kate by twenty years and had lived in Harrington Street for about the length of that time. Outwardly, the house was exactly the same as all the others in the street, but inside the porch were three bell pushes and three names. She pressed the bottom one next to the name Jameson.

There was a longer delay than she had expected.

If the old lady was out, would another ring disturb the

neighbours in the house? Did—

There was a flurry of footsteps, and the door opened and Mrs. Jameson stood there, her eyes bright as with tears, her grey hair untidy, her blouse sleeves rolled up to the elbows. Just for a moment, she paused, not recognising Kate; then, on recognition, she burst out: "Oh, the poor lamb, she's lost her baby! She's lost her baby! And the doctor's up there fighting for the poor lamb's life. I thought you were the ambulance, it's supposed to be here by now."

As if answering her, the ringing of an ambulance bell sounded in the distance; and at the same moment understanding of her own mood fell upon Kate Gideon like a thunderclap. She was twice appalled: by the awful thing that had been happening in this house while she had been going over her grievances – yes, that was what she had been doing: and by the subconscious power of her own thinking.

She and George had lost a child.

Not in childbirth, but soon afterwards. Not in this street, but in a top flat in a house not very far away. She had so desperately wanted George to come back, for she was fearful of being alone with the child, if death came. But George had been out, working; and she *had* been left alone.

She was not needed here and would only be in the way when the ambulance men came in. She asked, of course: "Could she help, do anything at all."

"No, no, Mrs. Gideon, the husband's upstairs with her and her mother's on the way. You're ever so kind, but—"

"Of course. Of course. I understand," Kate murmured.

The ambulance was pulling up as she reached the car. Ferris got in nimbly and drove off, Kate sitting beside him, her eyes closed, thinking and remembering. What a strange, painful thing to happen. How dreadful for the young mother, the father . . .

"The husband's upstairs with her."

"Policeman first, husband, lover and father afterwards."

When they were in the stream of traffic in King's Road, heading towards the West End, Ferris shot her a sideways glance of which she was conscious and which made her open her eyes and look at him. Now there was only his profile, set in concentration, for two sports cars were passing. Neither had a "Doctor's" notice on the windscreen. When they had gone far ahead, Ferris asked without looking round: "Is everything all right, ma'am?"

"It will be soon," Kate answered; and feeling that she owed the man some kind of explanation, she went on: "One of the young couples in Harrington Street were going to have a baby. Their first." Her eyes stung. "They lost the child and are worried about the mother."

Ferris's lips turned down at the corners. "Bad luck," he said, gruffly. "It's always a shock when something like that happens, especially these days. The doctors know so much but sometimes they don't seem to know a thing."

That was the moment when Dr. Jonathan Kelworthy watched as his golden-haired patient was carried out of her bedroom on a stretcher. Watching as tensely was the young, black-haired husband, so nearly a father, who had the look of the Southern European about him. As the golden hair vanished down the stairs the husband swung round on the doctor and said in an anguished voice: "It is your fault! You should have sent her to hospital. If anything happens to my wife I will kill you! Get that into your head, I will kill you!"

Outside, on the landing, Mrs. Jameson heard the threat, and wrung her hands.

8

2

GEORGE GIDEON

FOR George Gideon, it had been a very different kind of day from Kate's; different in mood and tempo and, consequently, in his attitude. He had been looking forward to taking Kate to dinner without telling her where they were going; looking forward to talking; even looking forward to trying to ease some of the pressures which he knew were on her mind, some psychological, some natural. He had not yet discussed these problems with her, and in the secluded corner he had reserved at Boulanger's they would be able to talk freely, without being overheard. Moreover at the Moon World Club, only a short distance from the restaurant, there was said to be one of the best floor shows London had seen for years.

"Topless, of course," said the superintendent who had divulged that piece of information at a morning meeting, "but clean as a whistle. I'd take my daughter almost anywhere today, knowing she'd probably been there before; but I'd take my wife and mother to this show."

The management had been told that Gideon and his wife might arrive, and a special table was already reserved for them. Yes, Gideon thought, he wanted this to be quite an evening to remember for Kate. At the back of his mind he had the feeling that she felt that her life was, in usefulness, ending; he wanted her to know that in more ways than one, it could be a new beginning.

True, the day had been too busy to allow him to think too much about it. Within minutes of getting to his office he had learned that a man on the run after shooting a police officer, had been caught; that one major bank robbery had been foiled and its perpetrators held, because of a squeak from an informer. There was particular relish in both of these because he, George Gideon, had been at the morning briefing alone. For some years the Deputy Commander, Alec Hobbs, had taken much of the briefing session and been first to get the news, but Alec was on holiday, and would not be back for ten days. He was in Australia, combining a little police business and a lot of pleasure. Engaged to marry the Gideons' youngest daughter, he visited police stations and Criminal Investigation Bureaux by morning when Penelope was rehearsing; spent the afternoons with her; and most of the evenings sitting and listening to her playing, marvelling that his future wife held magic in her fingers whenever she sat at the piano. Consequently Gideon felt himself to be completely back in harness, instead of sustaining the role of a kind of elder statesman. And at the morning briefings, when every senior officer in charge of an investigation came to discuss the case with him, he spent more time with old friends than he had in months; years. Perhaps of even greater value, he was able to study some of the younger superintendents, known better by Hobbs. He had long trusted Hobbs' judgment of men: and that trust was being fully confirmed.

Gideon, then, was extremely busy, and absorbed in what he was doing. The anticipation of an evening out with Kate added zest to all of this, and until the last minute it had not occurred to him that he might be late. For Hobbs most certainly had his uses, one of them being to take over if late calls which needed supervision at Commander level came in. Tonight, a call had come from a midland Federation Headquarters.

"George," the Commander of the Federation had said, "one

of the ugliest prison escapes has just been reported from Dellbank." Dellbank was perhaps the oldest top security prison in the country. "Two men escaped, and they killed a warder and later killed the driver of a car they stole. We think they're on the M1 heading for London, but we're not sure. And our only knowledge of the car is that it is a medium-sized one."

"Put your *Information* man onto ours and I'll brief them to give this top priority," Gideon said.

"Thanks. Can I call you later?"

"I'll leave word where I can be found," Gideon promised, with a picture of Kate in his mind's eye.

He dialled *Information* on the inter-office machine, gave instructions, then stood up and went to his window, which overlooked the Thames, Westminster Bridge, the Embankment and, across the river, London County Hall. Traffic was massed everywhere, gaily-beflagged ships and boats sailed in bright sunshine up and down the river; it was a beautiful evening. Big Ben, out of sight but within hearing, struck six, and he turned back to the desk and gave instructions to the car pool to send for Kate; then on second thoughts, told the driver selected to come and see him.

It was Harold Ferris.

When Ferris had gone, Gideon left the office and walked along the wide, bare-looking passages of the Yard, heading for the lifts and *Information*. Only when he walked was he seen at his best and most powerful. A tall, very big man, with massive shoulders only slightly rounded, he walked erect but thrustingly, as if he would allow nothing to stand in his way. He had a strong face, rugged more than handsome; a face which, if carved in stone, would be memorable for its strength. His eyes were a steely grey, matching in colour the thick waves of his hair.

He found *Information* already busy.

The motorway, M1, was being closely patrolled and two road blocks had been put up. Provincial as well as Metropolitan police were working closely together. Prints of recent photographs of the two wanted men were being distributed, and two were pinned up on the notice board of the Chief Inspector on duty. Gideon read:

George Pitton – sentenced to ten years imprisonment for robbery with violence. Seven years to go.

Arthur Dalby – sentenced to life imprisonment for rape and murder of a fifteen year old girl.

"Pitton looks as if he comes from the stone age," the Chief Inspector remarked, looking at a simian-faced man with hair growing very low on a low forehead. "But Dalby—"

Gideon studied the photograph of the rapist killer, noting the remarkable good-looks, the kindly expression: it was almost impossible to imagine a man with such a face committing the crimes that he had committed.

"I see what you mean," he said. "Sent these to television studios?"

"Not yet."

"Get them over. And as soon as you can, get copies sent to the Back Room for the Press."

"Any statement, sir?" The inspector, a youngish man, was obviously anxious to do exactly what Gideon wanted.

"Check with the Federation," ordered Gideon. "I don't see why a brief recital of the facts shouldn't be given, sprinkled with alleged and believed-tos – and certainly say they're believed to be heading for London on the motorway."

"Right, sir." The inspector was already at a telephone, while an elderly messenger came into the big, long room, with its teleprinters and its up-to-the-minute, country-wide communication system, carrying a box full of more prints of the two prisoners. Messages were coming in of reports that the two men had been seen; but there were likely to be hundreds of such reports, all false, before the night was out.

There was nothing more Gideon could do.

He told *Information* where he could be found for emergency messages only, and then sent for another car; the handiest was a Flying Squad car about to start out after suspects inside a jeweller in the Strand, only a stone's throw from Boulanger's. Gideon squeezed in the back with two other men. Walkie-talkie radio messages kept coming in, while *Information* kept up a stream of instructions. If any of the others were ill at ease Gideon put that right by saying into a lull: "Now I know I wish I were back on this job."

After a general laugh a man asked: "Were you actually in the Squad, sir?"

"Four years."

"You mean we've got a chance of getting where *you* are, sir?" another man quipped.

Gideon joined in the laughter, then heard another instruction from *Information*. "Bandits in the Strand now attempting to escape in dark green Ford Cortina down Northumberland Avenue."

The driver exclaimed: "Cut down Chandos Street and we'll cut them—" He broke off, obviously suddenly remembering the precious cargo they had in the car. "Plenty of others can—"

"Cut down Chandos Street," Gideon ordered.

The driver let his siren wail and then signalled a left turn and swung into the narrow street. As he did so, a green Ford Cortina came hurtling towards them. The Flying Squad man turned his wheel enough to avoid a head-on collision, the other driver swerving right, hit a traffic bollard, and crashed to a standstill. The driver was out and running fast towards the Embankment before the police car came to a shuddering halt alongside the wrecked Cortina. One of the policemen jumped out of the door across from Gideon and gave chase after the running man. A hundred people were standing and staring, and a taxi with its *For Hire* sign alight was only just behind.

"You chaps get on with the job and forget me," ordered Gideon. He was out of the car in a flash, and hailing the taxi. "I want to get to Boulanger's in a hurry," he said authoritatively.

"That is a police car and they were giving me a lift."

The taxi-driver looked at him with sharp interest. "Mr. Gideon, isn't it?"

"Yes."

"Didn't know you were still on the beat, sir!" The driver chuckled at his own joke and leaned out of his cab to open the rear door for Gideon, who only just ducked in time to save bumping his head. He sat well back, while the taxi squeezed past the wrecked car. As they turned into Whitehall Place and its gaunt mammoths of Victorian architecture, Gideon saw the thief who had got away collide with a man coming towards him; his pursuer was only a few feet behind.

So they got them all, he thought with deep satisfaction.

The sudden race and the collision carried him back over the years. His Flying Squad days had been among his most difficult – in fact, only seriously difficult days with Kate. On the Squad one had no hours, too little rest, no time for home life. How Kate had hated it! And how different things were now.

The taxi dropped him outside the entrance in the narrow street where Boulanger's had served Londoners for at least four generations; and, it was said, neither the inside nor the outside had changed very much, some of it not at all. There was a tiny bar, where he expected to find Kate; he hoped he wasn't too late, and a glance at his watch reassured him; it wasn't quite half past seven, and he was here first. He much preferred it that way. A pale-faced proprietor, a great-grandson of the founder, and the head waiter came forward to welcome him. As they talked, and Gideon watched the door for Kate, a telephone rang at the bar. A moment later the French barman called out:

"Is zere a M' Shideon, pliz?"

Gideon almost groaned as he took the receiver. If this really *were* urgent he might have to go, but he would fight it to the last. The thought made him smile grimly as he said: "Gideon."

"George, we've got one of them," a man reported, and only after a moment did Gideon realise this was the Federation Commander and he was talking about the escaped prisoners.

"The man Pitton. He was caught driving the dead man's car, the one which was stolen. We've no idea where the other man is yet, but if the way your chaps are working is anything to go by, we'll soon have him."

"Splendid," Gideon said. "I'm glad—"

"Excuse me, sir." A different man, the *Information* inspector at Scotland Yard, interrupted as the other was saying goodbye. "They caught all *four* of the men involved in the jewel raid in the Strand."

"Couldn't be better," Gideon said. "This looks like being our night."

"Can't be sure yet, sir," replied the *Information* inspector sententiously. "I think it's going to be a busy night. Two lorry loads of citrus fruits were hijacked from Covent Garden this evening, and—"

"I'll take reports of that in the morning," Gideon said, for at that moment the door opened and Kate came in.

She looked stunning, in an outfit which Gideon had never seen before, but a single glimpse of her expression, before she caught sight of him and smiled, told him that something had distressed her; this wasn't going to be the evening he had planned, and looked forward to so eagerly.

3

TÊTE À TÊTE

"HALLO, love," Gideon said, drawing her forward and kissing her on the cheek. "I thought you said you couldn't wear brown."

Her eyes lit up. "Do you really like it?"

"Very much," Gideon assured her truthfully. "I'm sorry I couldn't get home for you, but—"

"Don't worry," she interrupted. "It's good to be here." Again she smiled but without the fullness of heart he had hoped for. "Ferris wouldn't tell me where we were coming until we were actually in the street. Then I knew." She turned as the patron came hurrying, hand outstretched in welcome; he kissed her hand and then murmured, "*C'est impossible.*"

Mischievously, he added: "You must please tell me the secret of how to grow younger." It was as if he sensed that he must make some special effort to please her this evening; and Gideon thought she looked more genuinely cheered up than by what he had said. "Come, please – I have the special table for you."

The special table was in a corner and one step above the rest of the main dining-room. On one side was a carved wooden screen protecting them from the kitchen door and kitchen noises; on the other a rather attractive stained glass window, while the entrance was wide enough for them to see most of the restaurant with its gay atmosphere of a French hostelry. On the table were six red roses.

"If you will tell me what you would like to have for an *aperitif* I will arrange it," Pierre Boulanger promised. "And if you would like my recommendation for you, Mrs. Gideon, and for you, too, M. Gideon, I would suggest the *filet de boeuf en croûte*." He spread his hands, and smiled, and disappeared, keeping an unobtrusive but careful watch on them. Before her *filet* Kate chose an avocado with shrimps and a bland sauce; Gideon, a pâté which he never failed to enjoy. The service was immaculate; they were treated as royalty; the food was a gourmet's delight.

Yet, some air of tension remained in Kate.

Shall I ask her what it is? Gideon wondered, troubled.

I should have told him when I arrived, now it's more difficult, Kate thought. If I keep it from him he'll wonder why.

"Kate," Gideon said, as he waited for another slice of the pâté, "what is it? No bad news, is there?"

Hesitantly, she said: "No, not really." Then, realising the inadequacy of the reply she went on: "Not for us, that is." Now she could lead into the subject, knowing how quickly he would understand the effect of the child's death on her; for this huge man whom some thought dull and even insensitive had one of the quickest minds a man could have. That he had always possessed; but his sensitivity had grown slowly, over the years. "You know that the girl across at Mrs. Jameson's was going to have a baby, don't you?"

Gideon said in a surprised way, "Yes, of course."

"It was stillborn," Kate told him. "And the mother—well, Mrs. Jameson might be exaggerating but she implied that it was touch and go with the mother, too.

"When did you find this out?" Gideon asked.

"Only a few minutes before I left."

"And all the years rolled back and all the hurt was with you again," Gideon said. His big but well-shaped hand closed over Kate's, pressed gently, and stayed while the trolley was wheeled up and the silver hood was turned over, revealing a freshly cooked *filet en croûte*. The end cut looked temptingly appetising, but it seemed almost a sacrilege to over-indulge just now. The carver hovered, a waiter with the sauce hovered, each puzzled, until Kate said: "Darling, do you think I might have a tiny piece?"

Gideon stared, and then said: "Good lord, of course!" And the knife flashed and cut, while Kate turned her hand under Gideon's and gave him a strong, reassuring squeeze.

"Yes," she said. "The years and the pain rolled back, George, but so did some of the good things before and since. I wonder if—" She broke off.

"Yes?" Gideon watched her anxiously.

"It doesn't matter," Kate said.

"Nonsense. Of course it matters."

"That is enough, M'sieur? Or a leetle more?"

"It's fine, thanks."

"Madame?"

"Just what I wanted."

"Some haricots verts, madame?"

"No, just this."

At last the trolley was wheeled away and they were on their own again, Kate beginning to eat. "In a minute," her eyes said, and that suited him. Somewhere afar off the telephone bell rang and momentarily Gideon feared it was for him, but no one came. He saw Boulanger at the bar, talking earnestly. Was it imagination or was the Frenchman worried? Thought and sight of him faded, and Kate finished her morsel of the filet and began to speak while Gideon was still eating.

"I don't know why, George, but I've been"— She paused, groping for a word, and found one that would do—"unsettled, lately. Restless."

"And with Penny away and the house empty, you find that surprising?" Gideon asked, mildly.

"I *tell* myself that's what it is," she said.

"But you don't convince yourself," Gideon responded.

"Not really."

She leaned back, feeling as if a weight had been lifted from her, that her discontent was George's business now, and that she could trust him to cope with it. "I'm sure I need some other interest, but I'm not really sure what. I've been so busy for so long, and I suppose I'm not a natural do-gooder. I mean, working for the Red Cross, or muscular dystrophy, or—*you* know, don't you?"

"I know what you mean," he agreed. "I'm not sure but I think you have to start that kind of thing early." He finished eating and took another sip of the full-bodied red wine. "If you took an interest in them I'm sure Harrington Street dwellers would think you the best neighbour they've ever had."

"They might have, once," she admitted.

Gideon's eyebrows shot up. "And what's changed you?"

"I haven't changed as far as that's concerned," Kate replied. "At least, I don't think so. But the neighbours have. How many people do you know in Harrington Street today, George?"

Half frowning, he admitted: "Not many." After a pause he went on: "Very few, in fact. Half of the houses have been turned into flats, and a very different type of person lives there." He watched as one of the lesser waiters cleared the table, and went on slowly: "Are you driving at anything, Kate? Do you want to move?" When she didn't answer immediately he went on: "I could well understand it, the place is big and empty now, you must feel as if you're rattling around in it when you're there alone."

She laughed. "I do, rather."

"*Is* that what you want, Kate?"

"George," she said, "I honestly don't know. I don't think so. Oh, I don't pretend I haven't thought about it occasionally, moving out further *or* moving right into town, but things are pretty expensive at the moment."

"We'd get a very good price for the house," Gideon remarked, when she paused.

"Would you move, George?"

"Of course, if you wanted to."

"I don't mean that, I mean of your own accord, without any prompting from me, would you want to move away from Harrington Street? Be honest with me, darling – would you?"

He wanted to say roundly: "No," and that would be the truth. It was the last thing he wanted to do. But—"be honest with me, darling"—there were times for honesty, times for literal truth, times surely for half-truths. He wanted her to be happy. If she were not, he would not be. They were a long way from the evening of their lives but they were at cross roads; he could remember Winston Churchill in his war-time speeches using a word he had never heard before: climacteric, meaning a period of life at which vital force begins to decline. He would soon have more time and they ought to be able to use and enjoy it together, but he would be out and about more, she would by the very nature of their lives, be the home anchor. If she wanted to move from the house where they had been for so long then she must be free to move, but a round: "No!" from him would put invisible bars up at the windows and the doors of Harrington Street. All of these things passed swiftly through his mind, but not so swiftly that she was not aware of the silence.

"You'd hate to move, wouldn't you?" she said.

"No," answered Gideon, with great deliberation. He gave a smile, quick and warm, one which he contrived to keep entirely for her, and then went on: "But I'd hate to move and then find we wished we hadn't."

"I don't follow you!"

"We could let the house," Gideon said.

Obviously, the thought had not occurred to her and she was completely taken aback. Before she could comment, the waiters arrived with a lemon soufflé, known to be their favourite, and a gentle white wine brought with the compliments of M'sieur Boulanger. Kate was watching Gideon warily, while he was looking about for Boulanger, who would normally come, at this stage in the meal, to make sure that all was well. He appeared at the telephone again and there was now no question: he was worried.

"Let it *furnished*?" asked Kate, wonderingly.

"Or partly furnished," Gideon replied.

"Are you really serious?"

"I am wholly serious," he assured her, forcing his thoughts off the unknown troubles of the restaurateur so that he could concentrate on his wife. "I don't mean let's put it on the market tomorrow, but I do mean let us think seriously about living somewhere else for a year, even two or three, without getting rid of the house entirely. At the end of that time we would know what we really wanted, and wouldn't spend the rest of our lives regretting a hasty decision."

"You're quite right," she said, as a waiter hovered. "Are you going to have a brandy, dear?"

"Coffee, m'sieur, madame? Et le cognac?"

"I'm not sure," Gideon said, and put his head on one side. "Kate, would you like to go on somewhere?"

"Go on?" She was startled.

"Well, why not? One of my chaps tells me that a new show has opened at the Moon World."

"You mean a night club?" she exclaimed.

"Believe it or not, I mean a night club," Gideon said solemnly.

"George," declared Kate Gideon. "I don't think I'll ever get to know everything about you. I would *love* to go to a night club, and we can have coffee and a liqueur or something there. Is there any hurry? I'll have to tidy up, and—"

"There's no hurry at all," he assured her. "The first show doesn't start until half past eleven, and I've already arranged for a table. Take your time." He stood up, moving his chair so that she could pass more easily. She had hardly gone down the single step towards the cloak-rooms when Boulanger appeared, his expression not only worried but frightened. There could be no doubt that he had waited for the chance to have a quiet word with Gideon, but now that it was here he seemed tongue-tied.

"What is it, *mon ami*?" Gideon asked. The polite little

21

venture into French might help to loosen the other's tongue; the reminder that he was not simply a detective but that they had been good friends for many years; from the time, in fact, when a young Gideon had made an arrest in this very place but so quietly and with such little fuss that none of the diners had realised what had happened.

"Mr. Gideon," Boulanger said. "I am very much troubled. I do not know whether you can help me. If I should ask, you will forgive me, please."

"There's nothing you can't ask," Gideon assured him. "What is it? Something that has happened tonight?" He thought perhaps there had been a thief at work, in a cloak-room left unguarded for a few moments; or a clever pick-pocket discovered in the guise of a waiter. He thought in fact of virtually every possibility except the one which Boulanger now mentioned in a tone so low it was obvious he did not want to be overheard.

"Two of the people who have dined here tonight have been taken ill," he declared. "One of them is very, very sick, and in the hospital. Each of the customers had some eels, a very special delicacy, and each customer also had some pork. I have had the check made, Mr. Gideon. In all, seven customers ate those two things – just seven. Two I know. One of those in hospital I know. The others are strangers. If – and I must consider it – if this illness is poison from the food then the people I do not know should be warned. But—think of the consequences for the restaurant. Is there a way to enquire and warn them, M'sieur, and at the same time be discreet?"

"What makes you so sure the others will fall ill?" Gideon asked slowly, but his mind was racing.

"I am not sure. Simply, I am afraid. If I do nothing and others fall ill and die, what of my conscience? And such poison can affect some people in an hour or two, other people may not be affected for three, four, five hours. I cannot take the chance, M'sieur Gideon."

"No," Gideon agreed.

He saw Kate out of the corner of his eye and wished this had happened on any other night. He had no choice, however, no more than Boulanger, and he had so much less to lose than the little Frenchman. As Kate approached he reached one decision and said quietly to Boulanger: "I think if we name the kind of eel and where it comes from, and the shop from which you bought the pork, we can put out a call without bringing you in by name." He put out a hand to Kate, who needed no telling that something was wrong. "Kate," he said, "I have to talk to the Yard but it won't take long."

"You mean others, besides those who are here, could be affected?" Boulanger asked.

"Obviously it's possible," Gideon said. "And we can't find out too quickly. Will you explain to Mrs. Gideon while I talk to the Yard?"

4

NIGHT LIFE

GIDEON finished talking on the bar telephone to the man in charge of the Yard that evening, put down the receiver and rejoined Boulanger and Kate; Boulanger had got round to the subject of Penelope's piano playing; she had played a solo in a short presentation of Liszt on the BBC a few weeks ago, and he had heard it. So great was his courtesy that he did not turn too hurriedly to Gideon although he must be aching to hear what had been done.

"Calls for people who have eaten eels or pork anywhere this evening are going out on television and all radio stations," Gideon said. "Anyone who feels the slightest stomach cramping or nausea is being advised to go to a doctor or a hospital at once. I don't see what else we can do. And the two cases might be coincidental, I should try not to worry too much."

Boulanger put a hand to his forehead and said huskily: "Only one time have I heard of trouble with the Oise eels, M'sieur Gideon. Hundreds of people were made ill and some died."

"You don't often get epidemics of food poisoning as serious as that," Gideon said.

Outside, while the doorman went to get a taxi for them, a sharp wind blew and Kate shivered. Gideon slipped his arm round her. She leaned against him for a few moments, not solely for warmth, and he was almost sorry when the taxi arrived. The doorman opened the door for Kate, accepted Gideon's tip with a flourish and saluted as they went off.

There was a hint of laughter in Kate's voice as she settled herself. "A busy night for Commander Gideon."

"You don't know how busy," Gideon said, and told her about the Flying Squad case. Almost as soon as he finished he wondered whether he should have done; she murmured something which he didn't quite catch, but he did not press her to repeat it. Soon, they were in Soho, and approaching the Moon World Club, passing the inevitable crowds of tourists, striptease and topless show touts, the pimps, the narrow doorways with their post-card announcements of French massage and off-beat sex attractions. The gay lights crossed and recrossed Kate's face and she was gradually won from her thoughts to the scene of Gideon's square mile: Soho, and the streets nearby. It was some time since he had been here, and ages since he had brought Kate. The taxi slowed down and Gideon said: "There'll be one more message for me here. That should be the lot."

"When the evening's over I might believe that," retorted Kate.

The Moon World Club had a narrow entrance, the doorway festooned with lighted moons, crescent shaped, half-moons, full moons, even a few with female models whose breasts were made to look like the full moon with the man in the moon winking at the passers-by. But if the entrance was cheap and tawdry the foyer was of a fair size, the photographs on the red-papered walls of modern-day singers and pop stars. At the foot of a staircase covered in thick, rich carpet and which grew wider the lower they went down, a youthful-looking man in a dinner jacket and black tie came forward.

"Commander Gideon?"

"Yes."

"I am Charles Todd, the manager here. We're very glad you can be with us. I have a message for you. Your office would be grateful if you will call them, Commander. There is no hurry," he added. "We will delay the start of the show if necessary. What will you have to drink, Mrs. Gideon?"

Kate watched George disappear into a room marked "Private". If he hadn't warned her about the call, she thought, she would have been as mad as a hatter, as it was she was resentful; they, the nebulous "they" of the police, could not leave him alone for five minutes.

George was gone only for a very short time, and she thought there was more spring in his step as he crossed to her.

"I had the Yard check with the hospital about Mrs. Moreno," he said. That was the name of the young girl who had lost her baby. "She's holding her own and the chances are very good. And the hospital wouldn't lie to the Yard, love." A great wave of affection welled up in Kate, and overflowed, encompassing this man who, among all his preoccupations, had taken the trouble to find out the one thing she longed to know. Not once again that evening nor in the early hours, did the restless mood return. She looked on indulgently as he watched the stage and roared with laughter at jokes both childish and sophisticated. It was much more than a night club show, much nearer a musical; and if the dancers wore no more than G-strings and an occasional ostrich feather, there was a certain forthrightness about it that disarmed criticism. As Gideon finished the last of a bottle of champagne and called for his bill, the manager appeared.

"I hope you'll be our guests, Mr. Gideon."

"Not for as long as I'm in the Force," Gideon said. "But thank you all the same."

The bill came and was much smaller than he had expected, but was this an occasion to make a fuss? He followed the crowd out, Kate close to him, and as he reached the narrow street and stood beneath the moon-lit doorway, a doorman pushed forward.

"Your car's here, sir."

He hadn't ordered a car, and hesitated.

"Mr. Gideon," the manager said from his side, "it is my car, and I won't need it for at least half-an-hour."

It was very quiet in the bedroom.

Kate lay still and he wondered whether she was asleep, or pretending; whether, lying with her back to him, she was looking at the light in the attic flat across the road. Whether she would welcome his hand upon her bosom; whether this was a night for gentleness and quietness and sleep. The clock in the front room downstairs struck two, and he would have to be up by half past seven and off by half past eight.

Her voice came sleepily: "George, tomorrow's Friday."

"I know," he said, surprised.

"We're near the weekend. Can we—oh, I'd forgotten, of course we can't."

"Can we what?" he insisted.

"Go away for the weekend, somewhere not too far? On the river, perhaps, with a room overlooking it. I'd forgotten Alec was away."

"I had weekends off before I'd heard of Alec Hobbs," he said, drily. "If anything prevents us, it's going to be very serious indeed."

She put a hand out to cover his; and very soon he felt her arm go limp and knew that she was asleep, he was going to prove nothing to her tonight; unless this had been the best proof of how he felt towards her. He drew his hand away carefully and eased over on his other side, where he had learned to sleep so that if the telephone bell rang he could simply move his left arm over and pluck the instrument up before Kate did more than stir. He stifled a yawn and expected to drop off to sleep soon—but he did not. He found himself going back in his mind to the night when he had been forced to choose between staying with Kate or doing his job, his "duty" was the more formal way of putting it. There really had been no choice. Occasionally he wondered whether, even today, Kate realised that: really understood it; and whether the time had come when in her heart she had forgiven him.

Which was the more important? Understanding or forgiveness?

Could one, over the years, have one without the other?

A creak in the floorboards made him suddenly more alert, and when he had satisfied himself that the noise was no more than that, his thoughts were off on another track. None of the Flying Squad men tonight had hesitated to take a chance which might have led to a serious, even a fatal collision with the bandits' car; and in these days of increasing violence all of them must have known that the others might be armed. The police had responded almost in a reflex action; thank God, so had he!

The balance on this particular day's police work seemed good. The fact that a rapist and a killer was at large was on the debit side but at least the whole Force could concentrate on that man. There was no major hunt on, apart from that, at the moment: a thousand criminals on the wanted list, but that was normal.

What were they planning, these criminals, and others as cunning, or more so?

That was a question which often struck him with great force. Someone had plotted the jewel raid this evening; Pitton and Dalby must have been planning their escape for a long time, no doubt with help from fellow prisoners. And – a strange thing to enter his mind, except that in its present receptive mood almost anything was likely to pop in and out of it! – there was that lorry load of citrus fruit stolen from Covent Garden Market. No thieves would steal such a load unless they had a market all ready; one didn't go round trying to find a vendee for such goods. So, where were these going? A point to remember: they would have to be sold soon or they would be worthless, unless they had been in a special van at exactly the right temperature, and nothing had been said to him about that.

It wasn't a thing to worry about now; by the time he reached the office, the lorry might have been discovered.

Vaguely he thought of Boulanger and the two poisoned customers, wondered if by chance each could have eaten the offending food before getting to Boulanger's, thought more vaguely that he was glad neither he nor Kate had eaten the eel and the pork, or the eel *or* the pork for that matter; and at last he fell asleep.

So much was being planned, or was being born in the mind of man, that would cause trouble or at least activity for the police.

At the hospital where Daphne Moreno lay inside an oxygen tent, looking near death, her husband Paul kept muttering to himself, although the nurse who was constantly in the curtained-off section of the ward could not distinguish the words. Even if she had done so, she would not, in all probability, have taken them seriously, for he was distraught, she told herself, and tired to a point of collapse.

"If she dies," the young husband muttered, "I'll kill him."

Jonathan Kelworthy, in a twin bed next to his young wife, could not sleep. He was too unpractised in his chosen vocation to be able to throw off the effect of the death of that child. How had he come to lose her? Why, of all the tens of thousands born each week, had that soft-skinned, gentle girl been so robbed? Was it some error of his, of commission or omission? He went through every stage of his treatment of her and could think of nothing, nothing at all. He would check each step in the morning, and talk to Sylvester about it: Sylvester was the obstetrician who was counsellor and friend to youngsters like himself.

He pushed the bedclothes back slowly and cautiously, and crept out of bed. The springs creaked. He watched Janice, not wanting to wake her, because—oh, never mind, because. He must go downstairs, warm some milk and have a biscuit; that might break his obsession with the stillborn child, the dangerously ill mother and distracted father. He was halfway

29

to the door when he heard Janice turn in bed, and then call in a voice heavy with sleep: "What's the matter? Have you had another call?"

"No," he answered. "I'm restless, that's all. I'm going downstairs for a few minutes."

Her voice came again, a little contemptuously. "You're a fool if you're worrying about that Moreno girl and her baby. If you ask me, you had more than a soft spot for that patient."

How the words, the implication, hurt.

How right and yet how dreadfully wrong she was!

Of course he had a soft spot for anyone who was weak and helpless from sickness. That was why he was a doctor. But Janice would never understand. He was sure of that now. Janice wanted the social prestige of being a doctor's wife but no part in being his wife, in the sense of helpmate. He had been facing that truth for months now.

He said quietly: "You go to sleep, darling," and went out, half afraid that she would pursue the subject; but obviously she was too tired, for when he came back she was fast asleep. He stood looking at her for a few moments, a pretty – no, damn it, a beautiful face which showed at its best in the light filtering through from the streets.

She looked—pure.

He thought: "If I'd dreamt you would be like this . . ." and then checked himself, and went back to bed.

Arthur Dalby, quite unaware that his co-escaper had been caught, slept in the car which he had stolen. It was parked in the garage of an empty house. Like Janice Kelworthy, his face and expression looked "pure". Every now and again he smiled in his sleep.

Not far away from him, at a wholesale fruit and vegetable warehouse on the outskirts of Birmingham, four men unloaded a lorry load of oranges, grapefruit and lemons, all of which had come from South or West Africa. They did the work quickly, but without secrecy; night unloading was not uncommon here, for there was an open market nearby which had to be kept fully supplied, as well as the dozens of small shops in the south-east Birmingham area. When at last the truck was empty, money changed hands: two hundred and fifty pounds in small, used notes.

"Now all we've got to do is ditch the lorry," said the driver to his companion. "Then we've got a hundred each and fifty in the savings account!"

For some reason, that made him roar with laughter.

5

POISONING

KATE was asleep when Gideon woke, and he did not disturb her, but made himself a pot of tea, then bathed and shaved in the bathroom along the landing, and, that finished, stood outside the bathroom door looking at a loft ladder which disappeared into a partly open ceiling hatch. This led to the soundproofed attic, where Penelope *was* to have practised. He remembered the extreme excitement when he had promised to have this done, because so many neighbours complained about her practising classical music at all hours of day and night. It had been an expensive job, but for one reason or another, mainly the fact that she had been away with the BBC Symphony Orchestra so much and partly because she and Alec Hobbs had needed some time together, the Bechstein Grand hoisted up before the attic had been refloored, had seldom been used.

A case of Gideon's Folly, he thought wryly, then shaking off his nostalgic mood, strode purposefully downstairs. He could get breakfast at the Yard canteen and would be there in twenty minutes. He stepped out into a morning with a wraithlike mist covering grass and shrubs and trees, and obscuring the sky, but there was a promise of a warm day. The doctor's car was not across the road, and all the blinds at Mrs. Jameson's house were drawn; she was a great believer in savouring grief to the full. For once he had not underestimated the crush of traffic as he drove along the Embankment, and he was in Parliament Square in fifteen minutes; it took another six or seven to reach the Yard itself.

Men who saw him seemed to pay him more attention than usual; one actually saluted, and that puzzled him. Respect he was used to, but not deference. He went up two flights of stairs and into his own office, where several files had already been placed; Hobbs or no Hobbs, the system went on. A youngish Chief Inspector with the hard-to-believe name of Tiger was standing-in for Hobbs, and would come the moment he was summoned.

On the desk were four newspapers, folded so that only the front page headlines showed. He rounded the desk which was at one side of a medium-sized room with a big window overlooking the Embankment, desk, chairs and filing cabinets of rich-looking red mahogany, and snatched up the papers.

GIDEON CATCHES BANDITS!

COMMANDER GIDEON IN CAR CRASH — THIEVES CAUGHT.

YARD CHIEF IN LONDON CHASE.

BRITAIN'S TOP DETECTIVE IN CHASE AFTER BANDITS.

And on every front page his photograph stared up at him.

"The fat-headed idiots," he growled, and then opened the papers full out. He was relieved to see photographs of the Flying Squad men on the inside pages, though exasperated that they were considerably smaller than those of himself. There was also one of the crashed car.

His internal office telephone rang and he picked it up and growled: "Gideon."

"Good-morning, Commander." There was no doubt who this was: Sir Reginald Scott-Marie, Commissioner of the

33

Metropolitan Police, one of the few men who made Gideon leap, metaphorically, to his toes. Usually the "Commander" meant that there was someone in Scott-Marie's office, to prevent him from the "George" which had become more customary, but something in Scott-Marie's inflection told Gideon that this time it was out of good humour, rather than formality.

"Good-morning, sir."

"So you've reduced yourself to the ranks," Scott-Marie remarked.

"Next time I get a lift in a Squad car I'll be more careful," Gideon said.

"So that's what it was."

"As simple as that," Gideon said.

"Well, you obviously hit the headlines," declared Scott-Marie genially, "a welcome boost to police morale." He paused, and when he spoke again there was a subtle change in the Commissioner's tone, a seriousness. "George, what made you start the food poisoning enquiry last night?"

"I was dining at Boulanger's," answered Gideon, astonished that Scott-Marie should know of it.

"One Cabinet Minister was dining at Les Gourmets in Chelsea," said Scott-Marie. "He had those River Oise eels, and he's a very sick man. Not fatally ill but ill enough. I had one of his colleagues on to me as soon as I got in this morning."

"The Home Secretary, I suppose," Gideon said.

"Yes. He had been told by one of the divisional superintendents that there was a general enquiry, emanating from you." Gideon grunted. "It looks as if that particular consignment of eels should be traced, doesn't it?"

Scott-Marie did not often make positive proposals unless he was consulted, and Gideon read into this one the probability that the Home Secretary, who was Minister in charge of Home Affairs and therefore of the police, was exerting some pressure.

"I'll check," Gideon said. "If it's widespread—the food poisoning, I mean—then it should have been."

"Let me know one way or the other," said Scott-Marie, and then changed the subject completely. "How are you managing without Hobbs?"

"Managing," Gideon replied, drily.

"I had a letter from a colleague in Sydney this morning," said Scott-Marie. "He was very impressed"—Gideon expected him to say "by Hobbs" and not surprised but a little puzzled as to why Scott-Marie should choose this way of saying so—"by your daughter's playing," Scott-Marie finished.

"Good lord!" exclaimed Gideon.

"Apparently the leading New South Wales police turned up in force to hear her play," explained Scott-Marie, "and they gave a reception after the performance to the orchestra, Penelope being the star turn. She is a remarkable young woman, George."

"I couldn't agree more," Gideon replied.

When Scott-Marie rang off he, Gideon, replaced the receiver very slowly, and stared out of the window, filled with thoughts both happy and sad of a daughter twelve thousand miles away. Then he gave himself a little shake and turned briskly to the newspapers. Folding them neatly, he put them aside; he could read the articles later. Now he looked for the first time at the files. Big Ben began to strike. Ten o'clock already? He raised his head and counted . . . seven, eight, nine. *Nine.* He was in much earlier than he had expected, and Scott-Marie must have been at his office much earlier, too.

There were four folders, and the top one was very thin. He opened it, and saw a pencilled message heading several other messages, some of them teletyped. This message said:

Mrs. Moreno died at seven-twenty this morning, August 26th, at St. Stephen's Hospital.

At that moment Paul Moreno was standing by the empty bed in his wife's room. His dark eyes were ablaze, with anguish, with grief, and with hatred.

He said as if it were part of a refrain: "I shall kill that doctor. An eye for an eye, a tooth for a tooth, a life for a life."

"Jonathan, you are worrying yourself unnecessarily," Dr. Sylvester said to Dr. Kelworthy. Sylvester was an alert-looking man in his early fifties. He wore grey tweeds, and looked as hard and fit as a man could be. "There *is* no way in which we can guarantee a live birth. I've seen the child, of course, and I will do the autopsy on the mother, but I am sure you will find that there were some special circumstances and that you are in no way to blame."

Jonathan Kelworthy ran his fingers through curly, nut-brown hair, then drew those same long, strong fingers over his lean, attractive face.

"I hope to God you're right," he said. Then after a pause he went on: "I ought to go and see the husband. He needs sedation badly, and—oh, hell! I've got to go and see him, anyway! "

He turned and left the great man's office.

Gideon put in a call to Kate as soon as he had read the report, and then opened the next one. For some reason Hobbs' stand-in was not putting a description or name or title of the case on the outside of the folder, to Gideon an odd omission. He saw that this was the report on the food poisoning, and read almost unbelievingly:

Twenty-seven cases of food poisoning, at least eleven of them acute, have so far been reported in the Metropolitan area and its immediate environs. Two of the victims have died. Officers from the Yard as well as all divisions affected have been instructed to warn all restaurants not to use this particular eel. A list of wholesalers and shops and restaurants which deal in it is being compiled. There appears some possibility that the poison becomes more virulent when the eel has been eaten at the same meal as pork.

"Two dead!" exclaimed Gideon, and stretched out for the internal office telephone, but before he touched it, the bell of the Yard's exchange rang. Who—of course, Kate. He picked up this receiver, and the operator said: "Mrs. Gideon, sir."

"Kate," Gideon began, "I felt that I ought to tell you—"

"She's dead," Kate interrupted, in a very still voice. "I heard half-an-hour ago, George." Both were silent for a few moments before Gideon said: "There's so little to say."

"There's nothing, really," Kate said, "but I'm glad you called. Thank you, George." She sounded formal but no formality was intended, just a measure of her understanding of his concern for her. He wondered if he should tell her about the food poisoning and decided that it would only depress her more, and was actually about to ring off when he remembered what Scott-Marie had told him about Penelope. "Kate!" he cried, "don't ring off. I must tell you! Scott-Marie had a letter about Penny . . ."

He hoped that the good news would sustain her for the rest of the day.

What was he talking about? Sustain her for the rest of the day? Did he really think she was in such urgent need of support? Surely last night had been more of a passing mood than a constant or chronic one. He began to think about what they had said to each other, until suddenly he forced himself to dial Scott-Marie's office. Scott-Marie himself answered at once: "This is the Commissioner."

"That food poisoning looks very ugly," Gideon said, and for the sake of clarity, read out the report. Scott-Marie did not comment at first and Gideon went on: "So you can be sure we'll see that supplies are brought in. The divisions will work closely with the Health Departments concerned and I'll have a word with someone at the Ministry of Health to make sure there's not too much red tape."

"If you have any trouble let me know," said the Commissioner. He did not add, but obviously meant, that he would, if necessary, talk to the Home Office.

Gideon turned to the next file, his thoughts still on food poisoning. Why didn't Tiger put the name of the case on the outside of the files? Gideon flipped the cover over: this was about the prison escape case, and the summary was as brisk and lucid as he could hope for. He pressed the bell-push at the side of his desk which rang a bell in Hobbs' office: one ring meant come in, two meant, telephone me. Almost as soon as he had moved his finger from the bell-push the communicating door opened, and Chief Inspector Tiger came in. He was a big, muscular man with a benign expression. Anyone less tigerish it would be hard to imagine.

"Good-morning, sir."

"Good-morning, Chief Inspector. Explain a little mystery for me, will you?"

"If I can, sir."

"Why don't you put a description of the case on the outside of the folder?" asked Gideon.

For a moment, Tiger looked nonplussed, and he actually echoed "folder" as if he had been repeating Gideon's words to himself, one by one. Then the expression in his dark eyes changed to comprehension and he began: "Because I always"— but suddenly he stopped, obviously doubting the wisdom of what he was about to say, and added lamely: "I always thought you would like to name the case yourself, sir."

"Oh," said Gideon. "Did you?" What this man meant, of course, was that Hobbs liked to use his own phraseology; it was always Hobbs' writing on the outside of the folder. "Well, pencil a description in, in future, and if I don't like it I'll change it."

"Very good, sir."

"Has anything else come in during the past half hour or so?" Gideon asked.

Tiger did not hesitate this time, and the answer came quickly.

"I think so, sir. It may be coincidence but I rather think we're up against something new. A refrigerated meat container lorry was hijacked on the M1 this morning. That's the third somewhere in the country inside a month. And the lorry taken from Covent Garden last night, full of oranges and grapefruit, was found empty in a disused quarry outside Coventry two hours ago. *Some* one must have had a ready market for that kind of fruit, sir—and *some* one must know where they can sell that meat in a hurry."

6

MURDER ONE

GIDEON sat very still in his chair for what seemed a long time. Tiger stood in front of the desk, silent now, perhaps wondering whether he had said too much. If Gideon had a criticism of the man it was that he had obviously had this in his mind for some time, days at least, but had not uttered a word about it; probably he would have spoken to Hobbs.

At last, Gideon said: "Have you done anything about this?"

"I don't understand you, sir."

"Have you told anybody else what you suspect – the big market security police, for instance?"

"No, sir," replied Tiger.

The obvious rejoinder was: "Why not?" but Gideon had a feeling that he must not let this man feel the sting of criticism too early. One worked *with* the men as much as was practicable, not above them. "I think we should," said Gideon. "I think we need a breakdown on the thefts from the London markets, anyhow – Smithfield, Billingsgate and Covent Garden. It might be possible to tighten up security at some of them." He saw eagerness in the other man's eyes as he went on: "It looks as if the goods are taken out of London and sold in the provinces. Thought anything about that?"

"I really only woke up to the full possibilities last night,"

Tiger admitted, "but once I started to think things over, a lot of bells began to ring at once. As the goods are all perishable they'll want to get rid of them quick. They might steal a refrigerated truck but I doubt if they'd be able to maintain temperature control for long. And they would expect the lorries to be missed pretty soon, so they'd want to be out of London in a hurry. I'd say probably the M1 up as far as Birmingham but no further north, sir. Of course they might have a lot of small vans waiting, so that they could spread the load, but if a refrigerated lorry or a special fruit-carrying one was seen in the same place, unloading into small vans, it would soon be noticed. There'd be a big risk, anyhow. So I'd say they have a big wholesaler ready to take the stuff at one go. The wholesaler could sell it in small lots without any trouble."

Tiger said all this very quickly as if to make sure Gideon couldn't interrupt. When he had finished he was breathing hard. Gideon nodded.

"That seems to add up. We need a man to get moving quickly, preferably one who's had some dealings with the Federation and the County people—"

"May I make a suggestion, sir?"

"Yes."

"Someone who knows the markets might be better in the long run. They can all get along with the provincial blokes if they obviously know their business."

"Ah," said Gideon. "Yes. Whom do we have?" He knew whom he would select unless the man was deeply involved in another case from which he should not be moved, but wanted to find out whether Tiger would select the same man, or had some special candidate of his own.

"Chief Inspector Cockerill, sir."

It was the man of whom Gideon had thought; one who had probed into thefts from Covent Garden two or three years before, but thefts on a much smaller scale than the present ones.

"I'll talk to him," Gideon said. "What's he on at the moment?"

"The Covent Garden job – I put him on to that at once. You weren't here, sir, and he seemed—"

"You were quite right to put Mr. Cockerill on the Covent Garden enquiry," Gideon told Tiger. "But get him here as soon as you can, will you?"

"Yes, sir."

"What about the food poisoning?" Gideon asked.

"That's a different kettle of fish," said Tiger, and looked puzzled because Gideon grinned. The pun dawned on him a moment later. "I *see*, sir. It looks as if it's confined to London, and probably the West End – Central London, anyhow. I asked Superintendent Firmani if he'd look after it for the beginning, sir."

"Why Mr. Firmani?" Gideon wanted to find out how this man's mind worked.

"Well, chiefly the lingo," replied Tiger without a moment's hesitation. "The chefs and headwaiters at so many of these places may speak fairly good English, but as likely as not they're not fluent, especially those who work in the kitchens. Mr. Firmani's a pretty good linguist, sir."

"Right," Gideon agreed. "I'd like to see him, too."

"I'll arrange it, sir."

"Thanks," Gideon said in an obvious tone of dismissal, and he waited until Tiger reached the communicating door before saying: "Oh, Tiger."

"Sir?"

"I'm not going to miss Mr. Hobbs as much as I thought I was."

The other man actually turned a dusky red. He muttered something that sounded like: "Thank you, sir," and went out; the door closed very quietly. Gideon half-smiled, half-frowned, and turned back to the reports, to read each one thoroughly so that he was fully up to date. Those which Tiger had either written or edited were models of lucidity; some of the others were fuzzily-written, it was amazing how badly some first-class senior officers wrote their reports. But all of them gave him the facts, and facts mattered most, he could make his own interpretations.

The reports finished, he read the newspaper articles. They were exaggerated where his part was concerned, he had been used as the peg on which to hang the story, but a picture of the courage of the Squad car crew came through. Scott-Marie had referred to one man's comment in reply to the question: "Did Commander Gideon take charge?"

"He just told us to get on with it and never mind him," the detective had answered, and that was as good a summary as Gideon would ask for. Moreover, it underlined the fact that the men at the Yard were looking on him with approval. He was astonishingly lucky, and always had been, with his men, and their attitude towards him. When things had gone wrong their loyalty had been a byword. The feeling that he was one of them, that they were all dependent on one another, was perhaps the most important single factor.

Enough of self-congratulation!

His telephone rang and he picked up the receiver while writing on one folder: *The Markets Case.* "Gideon," he announced, and the operator asked: "Will you speak to Mr. Boulanger?"

"Yes," Gideon agreed at once, and thought: "I hope none of his clients died." Almost immediately Boulanger spoke, his French accent more noticeable on the telephone than when they had been face to face.

"Mr. Gideon?"

"Speaking," Gideon said in a quiet voice.

"Mr. Gideon," repeated Boulanger, "I have the news which is not good. First, M'sieur Harrison, who was at the restaurant, he has died. It is terrible, terrible." After a moment he went on: "There is another thing." There was a pause and Gideon wondered how many more of the people who had dined at Boulanger's had been taken ill. "The eels," Boulanger said stonily, "they were not from the right place."

"What?" Gideon's voice rose.

"You send a man, he asks many questions – a Superintendent Firmani, yes? I tell him where I buy the eels and the pork and he goes away. Afterwards, one of my assistants comes to me and tells me the truth. He did not buy the eels from the right place, which is a shop in Billingsgate – the market, you understand."

"I know what you mean," said Gideon.

"He buys from a man who comes to the back door when I am not in, and sells them cheap. They are not good and fresh, Mr. Gideon. They have been de-frozen, and then ice heaped upon them. I do not doubt they are the cause of the trouble. I would have told Mr. Firmani but he is not in."

"I'll see he's told very soon," Gideon promised. "Do you know the name of the man who sold you the eels?"

"There was no name given, it was a cash sale, Mr. Gideon. My man had so much to spend and he made the profit on the side, you understand. He is now very frightened and very ashamed."

"I dare say he is," said Gideon. "Will you hold him at the restaurant until Mr. Firmani has arrived?"

"But of course."

"Thank you," Gideon said. "And thank you for telling me. Goodbye." He rang off, and on the instant saw the handle of the communicating door turn, but it stopped at once and there was a sharp tap at the door. "Come in," he called, and Tiger appeared, a shadow behind him. "Mr. Firmani's here, sir, if you would like to see him."

"He's the very man I want to see," Gideon said.

Firmani always managed, somehow, to surprise him. The name implied an Italian or someone from Southern Europe, and Firmani was as blond as any Scandinavian, with a round face and a snub nose; everything about him was a contradiction to his name. He was a big man who moved jerkily as if operated by clockwork or by invisible strings; hence his nickname, Springer.

"Good-morning, Commander." There was a hint of Cockney

in his voice.

"Good-morning, Springer." The use of the soubriquet obviously pleased Firmani, who came across and shook hands. He was putting on weight. Gideon thought, and would soon have a sizeable paunch. He said pleasantly: "Sit down . . . I've just had a piece of news that should interest you."

"Who from?" asked Firmani.

"Boulanger. He just called me."

"He's been letting an assistant do the buying, and the assistant's been cutting corners in price," Firmani said, with evident satisfaction at Gideon's expression. "Am I far out?"

"Bang on, don't they say?" said Gideon. "Have you found others at the same game?"

"Commander," Firmani replied. "I have now seen the owners or managers of seven restaurants whose eels caused a violent form of ptomaine poisoning last night. Each of them either cut price corners himself or used an assistant who did. The eels as well as other fish were sold from a plain van which carried a small refrigeration unit which I suspect was there to impress, rather than to work. So far the descriptions of the driver salesman tally fairly well. Aged about twenty-five, fair-haired with hair growing back on his forehead, a broad nose and thick lips. I've got two of the restaurant buyers going through the rogues' gallery now – photographs of itinerant salesmen and house-to-house salesmen with records."

"*Very* nice work," Gideon said. "All the descriptions are about the same, you say?"

"Near enough for us to get a good Identikit likeness if the rogues' gallery is a flop," said Firmani. "I've got a man over with some city chaps at Billingsgate, to see if they know the fellow, as well as at two or three smaller fish markets and wholesalers in the City. With luck I should have something to show you by the end of the day."

It wasn't like Firmani to count his chickens too soon, so Gideon simply said: "We can't get results too quickly. Did you know that a Cabinet Minister was one of the victims?"

"Did I! He'll have his photograph in as many newspapers as you did this morning! Don't go and throw your life away, Commander, will you?" He obviously meant the remark seriously. "Well, if that's all—"

The internal telephone bell rang and Gideon lifted the receiver with one hand and raised the other as a sign of dismissal to Firmani. But before the superintendent opened the door, Tiger said into the telephone: "Is Mr. Firmani still there, sir?"

"Yes," said Gideon, and raised his voice. "Springer, half a mo!"

"Both the men going through the photographs have identified the van driver," declared Tiger. "He's a man named Baker who's had three short prison sentences for peddling old bread that had been watered and re-heated, as well as selling stolen fruit and vegetables. Jack Baker," he repeated.

Gideon replaced the receiver, and turned to Firmani. "It looks as if we know who the salesman is. Don't lose a minute picking him up, will you?"

Firmani was already opening the communicating door.

Jack Baker, known to wife, mother and intimate friends as Jackie, had one besetting fault; perhaps it was even a sin. He loved to get something for nothing. "Buy cheap, sell dear," was his motto, and he could quote a dozen instances of millionaires who had made their money in exactly that way. He was, on the whole, a happy man. He ferreted out bankrupt stocks and slightly fire-damaged goods and even some which he suspected had not been honestly come by, and sold them door to door in different parts of London. He was a good-natured man, and although there was something sensual about his full lips and roving eye, he was not often unfaithful to his wife; and he was a good provider, not only for her but for his mother, whom he three-quarters supported.

When, a few weeks before, he was asked if he would take on a job as van driver salesman to high class restaurants, he had jumped at it. For among his attributes was a nodding acquaintance with both French and Italian. It did not take him long to learn the names of the special fish he was to sell, and being Jackie Baker it did not occur to him that there was anything wrong in taking fish out of an old refrigerator which had a small electric motor inside for sound effects, and pretending it had been under constant refrigeration. After all, he had sold many a baker's dozen of rock-hard rolls or loaves, soaked in water and then put in a hot oven to make them fresh for at least long enough to sell.

There was big money in it by his standards, too; he was making a hundred pounds a week!

He went, on the morning of the food poisoning investigation, to collect his van from the old warehouse where he parked it, free, by night. It was a small warehouse, filled with old crates and cardboard cartons, close to Billingsgate Market. He would go to a small wholesaler, named Bateson, for his morning supplies and be taking in the shekels within an hour. He did not trouble to secure the double doors behind him, as there was little wind; he could edge one of the doors aside with the van if one did swing to.

He was actually starting the engine of the van, a Hillman Imp, when not one but both doors swung to. Muttering under his breath he got out of the seat and went to the doors to open them; but neither would budge. He pushed harder, then placed his shoulder against first one side and then the other, exerting all his strength, but nothing yielded; someone had fastened the doors from the outside.

"What the hell are you playing at?" he called out angrily. "If this is a joke I don't think much of it."

No one responded; and he heard no sound.

He looked about him, with sinking heart, knowing that there was only one window in this section, which had been sealed off after one end had collapsed years ago. The window was not only too small for him to climb out of, but too high to reach. Puzzled, but aware that he was stuck here until whoever had

47

secured those doors came back, he yelled: "Open up, you flickers! I've got my work to do!"

He kicked at the door.

Simultaneously with the kick there was a flash from behind him; as if lightning had struck. He spun round, and saw fires blazing not in one but in a dozen places, on the old crates and among the cartons. In sudden frenzy he rushed forward in an attempt to quench the flames, but as he did so there was another flash and another dozen fires started.

That was the moment when he realised that he was being murdered; being burned to death. A split second later he began to scream and kick wildly against the solid, unyielding doors. Behind him the heat grew fiercer and the fire grew closer until first his clothes, and then the very flesh of his body began to burn.

But before that he was dead of suffocation.

7

MURDER TWO

JONATHAN KELWORTHY pulled his car into a parking space outside Mrs. Jameson's house, for parking was fairly easy by day. It was almost the very moment that the fire had started at the disused warehouse, some seven miles across London as the crow flies. He looked tired and haggard, but his movements were brisk as he walked to the street door of the house. He rang the top bell twice and the ground floor bell – Mrs. Jameson's – once, an arrangement he had made with the two women to identify himself without bringing either to the front door. Then he pushed open the letter-box and fished inside with a bent forefinger until he touched a piece of string on which a street door key was hanging. He pulled the key through, metal rattling on metal, and inserted it into the front door.

There was no sign of Mrs. Jameson, he noted with a sigh of relief.

He went up the first flight of stairs and passed a doorway in a wooden partition which divided the landing into two. Beyond was a self-contained, three-roomed flat, equivalent to the two smaller bedrooms and the bathroom at Gideon's house. Then he went up a very narrow stairway leading to the attic apartment.

The whole place was gloomy, because of partitions and

boarded up windows. The stairway, a strong ladder securely fastened to the wall but with a flimsy handrail, creaked loudly. He had tried to persuade Mrs. Moreno to stay with friends rather than have these stairs to climb in the late stage of her pregnancy, but he had not been successful.

At the top was a narrow landing and a locked door. Usually it would be open for him. Now there was no sound. He put a finger on the bell, and then hesitated. Both the husband and the mother were said to be here. Supposing they were asleep, it would be criminal to wake them, for his main purpose in coming was to make sure they were getting rest, particularly Moreno, whose face was like the face of a dead man.

Should he ring? If the ringing from downstairs had not disturbed them, was there any purpose in it? He had other house calls to make, and needed rest himself.

He turned, cautiously, on the narrow landing – and as he did so the door opened. Caught almost off-balance, he grabbed the handrail and turned to face whoever was standing there.

Was it Paul Moreno?

It was Moreno all right, wild and unkempt, his right hand holding a knife with a thin bright blade. Sunlight came in stealthily from a half-blocked window and shone upon them both. But neither the knife nor Moreno's expression gave Kelworthy the slightest warning. He thought vaguely that the man had been cutting something, bread perhaps; and he was quite sure Moreno hadn't slept and was desperately in need of a sedative.

He smiled in greeting, gently, trustingly, and then he saw the movement of the knife, pointing towards him, the sharp end on a level with his stomach. He saw not simply tiredness and grief in the other's eyes, but madness. That was the moment when he knew beyond all doubt what Moreno intended to do.

Moreno drew his lips back and said through teeth that seemed too tightly clenched for utterance: "You killed her. *I kill you.*"

Alarm seared through Kelworthy. He dared not step back

quickly, or he would stumble and fall down the stairs.

With sudden, terrifying speed the knife was thrust towards him. He flung out his left arm and a searing pain shot through it. He moved backwards, slipped, and began to fall. The last he saw of the knife was the light flashing across the blade.

That was all.

He was oblivious of Moreno standing and staring as he fell down the stairs, blood already welling out of the wound in his throat. He did not hear Mrs. Smith, his mother-in-law, demand: "What is it, Paul? Who—" And he did not hear her scream.

He did not see Moreno turn and slash at her with the knife as she slammed the door in his face. He did not see Moreno stumble down the stairs, the knife still in his hand.

Moreno saw Kelworthy's body on the landing below.

He held the knife poised as if about to thrust it into the man once again; then, seeing the blood, he decided that Kelworthy was already dead or dying. He flung the knife into a stair tread where it stuck, quivering, sprang over the body and ran downstairs. He kicked against something which gave off a metallic chink of sound, glanced down and saw a bunch of keys. *Car* keys: the keys to Kelworthy's car! He snatched them up and hurried outside, slamming the door behind him. The red sports car was right in front of the house and he went straight to the driving seat, pushed the key into the ignition, and turned. The engine caught on the instant. Seen by several people, none of whom saw anything out of the ordinary, he eased the car into position.

Across the road, at Gideon's house, Kate was in the kitchen, scrambling eggs for a late breakfast.

She did not even hear the sports car being driven away.

She felt much more contented this morning, and enjoyed reading about George's escapade without any great feeling of concern: she had lived with the fact that a policeman's lot was a dangerous one too long to be easily worried. After washing up, and because she felt in the mood, she put on the russet brown suit, took her shopping basket, and went to the end of the road for a bus. A taxi came along and in a moment of rare extravagance, she took it.

She had shopped for years in a part of Fulham which had changed in some ways out of all recognition. As she got out of the taxi at the entrance to the small shopping centre she usually patronised, she saw a huge banner across the front of one of the new stores, bearing the words:

THE BEST BUY IN LONDON

This was a Quickturn store, one of the chains, where the food *was* cheap. Huge posters in the windows showed prices which were anything from ten to twenty per cent below the private store where she usually went.

The only thing which kept her out of Quickturn was the mass of people inside. "Her" store had only had a few customers and a manager who looked troubled.

Superintendent Firmani left Scotland Yard feeling very pleased with himself. It was some time since he had been briefed by Gideon, not Hobbs, and Gideon had managed to convey the impression of a meeting of old friends. If that wasn't enough, there was the news about the van salesman, and it should not be long before he was picked up. Already, there was a general call out for him in the London area, especially the restaurant districts of the West End, the City, Knightsbridge and Soho. And the Superintendent in Charge of a division which included the docks area, had jumped at the chance of sending men round to Jackie Baker's home in Fiddle Street, Whitechapel.

Firmani headed for the East End; driven by a long-jawed bony-kneed, big knuckled detective sergeant named Ebony. The radio was left on and snatches of talk, instructions and reports drifted into the car. They went by way of the Embankment, past the old sailing ships where cadets still trained. Then on beneath the underpass at Blackfriars, driving steadily until the stench from Billingsgate Market filled the air.

"Slow down," ordered Firmani, and the driver slid towards the kerb and the cobbled pavement. As he did so a City of London police inspector got out of a car parked a few yards along. No one in either of the London Forces was really aware of the anachronism of there being a Force, completely autonomous and independent, in the middle of the district covered by the Metropolitan Police Force. The truth was that they had grown up with it, and accepted it. Both Forces worked together and here was evidence of it. The City man, Greerson, was in uniform. He came towards Firmani with a smile.

"Come to help me out?" he enquired. He was big, red-faced and jovial-looking.

"Come to ask if you've heard anything about Baker yet," replied Firmani. "I'm on my way to NE and his house."

"So far the answer here is a blank," Greerson said. "There's only one of the wholesalers seems to know him, and that's by accident. Hold your nose." He took it for granted that Firmani would want to come into the great Market, and Firmani jumped at the chance. An old man wearing a filthy cap was hosing down the cobbles of one of the entrances, and although he stood aside, water splashed over their shoes. Firmani had a feeling that it was done intentionally. He stepped into the great hall, with its high ceiling, the cubicles round the sides, the main selling blocks in the middle. Huge piles of block and crushed ice stood about, making the place as cold as a winter morning, so cold in fact that it seemed to nullify the smell of fish.

There it was, on stone benches, in crates marked: Gt. Yarmouth or Felixstowe, Looe or Avonmouth, Hull or Grimsby, all the fishing ports to the east and the south-west of London. Small lorries and vans were being loaded by porters who wore their flat hats, like solidified and black-painted boaters, as if they were featherweight, although to some they must have seemed as if they weighed a ton.

Firmani felt ice crunch beneath his feet, and nearly fell. Greerson steadied him. A short, astonishingly broad man wearing a black jacket and striped trousers came towards them with a little shrimp of a man whose "boater" looked far too big for him.

"Anything more for me, Mr. Pettifer?" asked Greerson.

"Depends what you call more," replied Pettifer cautiously.

"Superintendent Firmani, Mr. Pettifer, the manager here," said Greerson.

"How are you?"

"How'd you do?"

"Mr. Charley Peak," said Pettifer of the shrimp. "You tell them, Charley."

Charley began to speak in a voice so croaking that at first Firmani could not understand what he said, but gradually the import of it came to him. Charley was not a full time porter at Billingsgate: he was retired and "helped aht a bit". He also helped small shops and wholesalers out when their staff was short because of holidays or sickness. That was how he had come to know Jackie Baker, who had started to call at wholesalers for fish and specialities at the end of the day.

"Didn't know a bloody fing about fish," croaked Charley. "Didn't seem to 'ave no sense of smell. Strewth. I'd have dumped most of what he bought."

"Do you know where he sold it?" asked Greerson.

"Search me, Guv'. I only know he took it away in a plain van. Green it was, with the name of the people who had it before painted out." Charley appeared to have finished his statement, and then he added out of the blue, "Not the only one, neether."

"What do you mean?" demanded Greerson.

"Been several of the blaggers lately buying up old fish. Ought to be a law against it, that's what I say." He allowed this profound statement to hover, and then, struck by the enormity of telling the law there ought to be a law, he began to laugh; and the laugh sounded exactly as if he were choking to death.

This alarming cacophony followed the two policemen to the doorway through which they had come in. The old man with the cap had moved further away but as they approached he began to swivel round, turning the jet of water gradually towards them while strengthening the pressure. It looked for a moment as if they would be swamped, but Greerson jumped round, over the jet, and then made a bee-line for the old man, who backed hastily away, letting the hose nozzle droop towards the cobbles.

"Hallo, Smithy," Greerson said. "Ever heard of resisting a policeman in the performance of his duty?"

"I never was—"

"Or using an offensive weapon? That's a very serious charge."

"Offensive weapon my—"

"I could even work in abusive language," interrupted Greerson.

"A hose ain't no offensive weap—"

"You're out of date, Smithy." Greerson would not let the old man finish a sentence. "A water-hose is now considered to be a powerful weapon, both offensive and defensive. It's used to quell riots all over the world."

"I'm not no riot!"

"You'd be surprised," Greerson said, and he laughed. "My chaps and the Yard might be coming in and out of here for a few days, you be careful with that hose." He took a packet of cigarettes out of his jacket and when Firmani refused one, proffered the packet to the old man. "How's Maisie?" he asked casually.

The deep-set eyes set in a lined face worn to the consistency of leather by the years of fighting for a living, stared at him unwinking. After a while the man stretched out a hand as gnarled as the branch of an old tree. He leaned forward to take a light from Greerson, and then said in a gruff voice without any of the anger and resentment he had shown before: "Think I'd be working if she was still around?" After a pause he added: "Lorst her, two years ago. Bloody cancer."

"Oh," said Greerson, and he looked genuinely concerned. "I'm sorry, Smithy. Very sorry."

The old man nodded, and Greerson and Firmani turned

away. They were out of earshot of everyone in the market and within earshot of a distorted voice coming over a police car radio before Greerson said in a tired-sounding voice: "You can't keep track these days. If I'd known about his old girl I'd have gone to see him. Used to make a living stealing fish from the boats and the lorries, but he's past that now. Want to know something funny?"

The radio voice was very loud as they stood by the side of Firmani's car.

"I'll buy it."

"He won't claim an old age pension, won't take anything from Welfare, won't even take help from the Salvation Army. Independent old flicker." He gave a guffaw of a laugh, this big, insensitive-looking man, and went on: "They don't come like him any more. If a crook goes through a lean patch you find him on the dole!" Firmani found himself laughing, too, but suddenly his laughter and Greerson's faded as a voice sounded more clearly from the car.

"Fire in a disused warehouse at Whitechapel, near Brown's Quay, caused the death of a man as yet unknown. The fire is now under control. Arson is suspected."

There was a pause before the man from *Information* went on:

"Special message for Superintendent Firmani. Please contact Superintendent Lemaitre at NE Division. This is urgent."

The voice broke off, and only atmospherics sounded, until Greerson said: "You're within ten minutes of him – why don't you go straight on and I'll tell him you're on the way."

In fact it was fifteen minutes later when Firmani stepped into Lemaitre's office in a big old-fashioned building in the heart of Whitechapel. Lemaitre, tall, spare, bony, grey, sporting a red and white spotted bow tie and a green and white check suit, stood up with his hand outstretched, and said in exaggerated Cockney: "Wotcher, me old mate. Dunno what you've started, do you? That cove you're after, Jackie Baker, burned to a cinder in that warehouse, van and all. And it was arson, all right – got the fire boys on to it already."

8

SUDDEN PRESSURE

FIRMANI and Lemaitre stood and looked at the gutted shell of the warehouse. Here and there crates and cartons still smouldered, giving off a pungent smoke. The van was burned right out except for the driver's cabin, which had been protected by the old refrigerator, itself a charred box. The heat had cracked, but not shattered the windscreen. Police were in the cabin, one man taking photographs, one using grey powder in a search for fingerprints. The man climbed down when he saw Lemaitre.

"Wotcher got?" demanded Lemaitre.

"No doubt about it, sir – Baker's prints are all over the wheel. All over the cabin, if it comes to that."

"Anyone else's?"

"I haven't found any yet, si"We need some," Lemaitre declared. "Don't miss a thing, George." He turned away and grinned at Firmani showing good but wide-spaced teeth. "Talking about George, how *is* Gee-Gee?"

"On the ball as ever," answered Firmani.

"Ask him when he's coming out this way," Lemaitre urged. "I haven't seen him since the police ball." There was a nostalgic expression in the bright eyes, for Lemaitre had been Gideon's right hand man for many years, until changes in the structure of the Yard had given him a chance to come out here as the Divisional Superintendent. There was neither jealousy nor envy in him for Hobbs; but there was wistfulness at times.

"I'll do that," Firmani promised, but he was still looking at the sheet of canvas over what he knew to be a charred heap of ashes, all that was left of Jackie Baker. He had a feeling which he knew Lemaitre shared: this was not an unconnected incident; this was the beginning of a major case. He felt it, as it were, in his bones.

So did Gideon.

First, he had the news from Firmani by telephone. Next, he had a call from Gillespie, the Chief Fire Officer for London, who confirmed that the cause was arson; a quick combustible preparation known as Firex had been thrown, or shot through the window and had set the place on fire in seconds.

"The poor devil didn't have a chance," the Fire Officer said.

"Is Firex used much?"

"It's used commercially for quick combustion and it's also used when big stacks of rubbish have to be destroyed. It's easy enough to get from the manufacturers and a few wholesalers."

"Will you let me have a list of all you know?"

"I'll do better," the other said. "I'll let you have a list of all producers, suppliers and stockists; in London for a start, and then for the rest of the country."

"Thanks," said Gideon.

He rang off, and contemplated the file in front of him. A first-class restaurant buying cheap fish from an on-the-make salesman who saw no further than the end of his nose was one thing. But why kill this man, and use such hideous means, except to make sure that he could not talk?

Someone knew that the police would find him very quickly; and someone feared that he knew enough to give the police vital information about them. What could that vital information be? Almost certainly it was information about crime on a large scale; people didn't kill in such a way unless it was. The sense of uneasiness which Firmani also felt was very strong in him. He called Tiger on the inter-office machine and asked: "What's the news on Cockerill?"

"He hasn't reported yet, sir."

"The message that I wanted to see him went out, I hope."

"The moment I came back to my desk, sir." Gideon grunted, and was about to ring off when the other man repeated: "Sir." Gideon detected a note of urgency in Tiger's voice. What was the trouble now? he wondered.

"Yes."

"There is one other thing that's just come in, sir. Very nasty."

"Oh," said Gideon, and he thought: We've had everything "very nasty" that we want, not more of it, for God's sake. "What?" he asked, his mind still on the fire at the old warehouse. He did not know Baker himself but had heard reports of him; a fairly harmless little man who wanted life to be on Easy Street.

"You know Dr. Kelworthy, sir, don't you?"

"I know of him," Gideon replied, wrenching his thoughts away from the other problem. "Why?"

"He was murdered this morning, sir. Just an hour or so ago."

Gideon echoed, stupidly: "*Murdered?*" then asked, in wonder, "But why?"

"The husband—" began Tiger, and from that moment Gideon understood. He heard Tiger going on "The husband of the woman who died in childbirth, a man named Moreno, went berserk. He killed him with a carving knife, sir."

Oh, God. Oh, God.

Kate.

"Are you there, sir?"

"Yes." Gideon made himself speak firmly. "Have we got him?"

"No, sir."

"What?" Gideon roared, as if this were Tiger's personal responsibility.

"Apparently he raced out of the house and drove off in the

doctor's car, sir. Apparently—" Tiger, obviously, was nervous—
"the doctor often kept his car keys in his hand – but that's
guesswork, sir. It was an hour before we learned about it,
apparently the dead woman's mother went all to pieces and the
landlady, a Mrs. Jameson, was out shopping. Fulham is
handling the case, sir. There's a general call out for the car, but
as far as I know nothing's been reported yet."

"Let me know when it is," Gideon said, and rang off on the
other man's "Yes, sir."

Gideon sat still and solid in his chair.

It was one of the most awful things in his experience. Could
they not—could *he* not have spotted that the loss, first of the
long-awaited child and then of the cherished wife, had turned
the husband's mind? A thousand, a million minds placed under
the same awful strain would not have broken; this man's mind
must have been already close to breaking-point.

Kate must know by now.

He wanted to go to her, but it was impossible. He was not
even sure that he should telephone her. On her own she would
probably hold up well, but if he were to talk to her she might
break down. Suddenly, he thought: "Priscilla". She was his
married daughter, living in a London suburb with children of
school age; Priscilla might be able to go and see Kate for an
hour or two. He put in a call to her through the exchange and
then looked up the number of a Dr. Malcolm Henby-Kite, one
of the Yard's consultants on psychiatric and pathological cases,
a man often called on to give expert evidence of the state of
mind of a man charged with a grave offence.

A woman answered his call, bright and brisk: "Dr. Henby-
Kite's office."

"This is Commander Gideon. Is Dr. Kite there?"

The woman hesitated. "Well, Commander, he's with a
patient."

"Is it a matter of life and death?"

"No, sir."

"Mine could be," Gideon said. "Put me through at once,

61

please." The nurse did not argue and the exchange telephone did not ring, so there was no answer from Priscilla yet. His inter-office machine began to ring, and he picked it up with his free hand. "Gideon."

"I've just had word from Mr. Cockerill," Tiger said. "He's been up to Northampton, sir, and only just got your message. He's on the M1 and should be here by half past three."

Gideon looked at his wristwatch and saw that it was nearly two o'clock.

"Send him to me as soon as he arrives," Gideon said. "And have the canteen send me down something to eat. They know what I like." At that moment a mellifluous voice sounded in his other ear; this was Henby-Kite's, who had one of the most impressively gracious-sounding voices imaginable. Even in the witness box he talked as if judge and jury were patients who needed to be soothed and indulged.

"Good afternoon, Commander. How can I help you?"

"With a very quick off-the-cuff opinion given without the full knowledge of the facts," said Gideon, and startled Henby-Kite into a laugh which was rather less considered than his usual speaking voice. "I can but try, Commander." Gideon explained, with the lucidity born of long years of making sure that he was clearly understood; and he described what little he knew of Moreno and of the young doctor: the *murdered* doctor. The very thought made him wince.

"As far as I can, I understand," said Henby-Kite. "May I presume to guess what you would like to ask me?"

"Yes."

"Is the young man so demented that he might kill others?"

"Yes," said Gideon.

"Commander," Henby-Kite said in a firmer voice than before, as if he wanted to make sure that Gideon could not possibly under-estimate the significance of what he said, "if I were a mother with a very young child I would not like to meet this man now. If I were a young and pregnant woman, I would not like to meet him, either. I give you as my considered opinion that in these circumstances he could – I do not say he would, only that he *could* – be extremely dangerous. It goes without saying that if cornered by your men he might be very dangerous, also; on the other hand if cornered he might kill himself." Henby-Kite paused for what, in the circumstances, was a long time, and then went on: "I do hope I have made myself clear."

"Crystal clear," Gideon agreed, gruffly. "I was alarmed before. I'm terrified now. "

"I really think you have cause to be until that young man is where he can do no harm," said the psychiatrist. "Please don't hesitate to call me if you think I can help. If the young man is cornered, I might be able to reason with him where less experienced men or women could not."

"I understand," Gideon said. "Thank you."

He rang off, but kept a hand firmly on the telephone, as if he wanted to hold onto something. This was worse than he had anticipated. Now he had to decide quickly what to do. Warn all divisions, of course; step up the search for Moreno until it had absolute priority. That much was easy but—how? If the men knew the kind of crime Moreno might commit, then they might find that vital little extra to put into the search. The murder of a policeman; the murder of a child or of a mother-to-be – these gave to most of his men reserves of strength that they did not know they had.

But if he put the full story out it would reach the Press; television; radio. It was the kind of thing which could spread near-panic; the kind of danger which might seriously harm a woman in the later stages of pregnancy.

If he didn't put out the full story, then none of these women would be warned to take care.

This was a period when there was no active Assistant Commissioner whom he could consult. He might be wise to check with Scott-Marie, but that would simply be shifting responsibility, or attempting to. The longer he clutched the telephone, the more certain he became of what he must do. He rang for Tiger, who came in as quickly as Hobbs ever did, and asked: "Do you do shorthand?"

"Yes, sir."

"Then take this down, get it on the typewriter as roughly as you like and let me have it the moment you're through. It's a general call to London and Home Counties—" He broke off, with a sudden flare of hope. "Is there any news of Moreno?"

"No, sir."

"The car?"

"No, sir."

"Then take this down, and fill in the blanks for me. Quote. The search for Christian name Moreno wanted in connection with the murder of Dr. Jonathan Kelworthy in Fulham this morning must be given absolute priority. Moreno, known to be suffering severely from shock, can be anywhere in the London Metropolitan area or beyond. He was last seen at – fill in – in Harrington Street, Fulham, driving a red MG number – fill in. Experts fear that the double shock of losing his wife and stillborn child may make him attack young babies and their mothers or women obviously pregnant. A special watch should be kept in High Streets, shopping centres and supermarkets. Officers must use their own judgment whether to advise mothers with infants-in-arms or mothers-to-be to stay in the open or stay in the security of their homes. Wherever possible out-of-doors they should not be alone." For the first time since he had started to dictate Gideon stopped, and for the first time Tiger's pencil stopped on his note-book; apparently he had kept pace without any difficulty. Gideon stared out of the window and then went on: "Since Moreno has had no experience in evading the police it should not be long before he is apprehended, but until such time the search for him must be given absolute priority. Repeat: Absolute priority. Signed: George Gideon, Commander CID."

He broke off, motioning to the other man to get up, and said: "The last sentences are for Press and publicity. Get moving."

"Sir," said Tiger.

"Well?" Gideon demanded impatiently.

"The message could go out as it is, without any revision."

"So I should hope. But I want to check for any change of emphasis," Gideon said. But he half-smiled. "You've lost a line on that typewriter already!"

Tiger went out of the communicating door like a streak, and for the first time the door closed behind him with a bang.

Gideon felt the sweat spreading across his forehead and the back of his neck. He was undergoing the kind of pressure that he had not experienced for a long time; and until Moreno was caught it would get worse. But he must not let the other cases slide; he needed to concentrate on the food business, although that could wait until Cockerill arrived.

There was a tap at his passage door, and he called: "Come in."

The door opened slowly and an elderly man, one of the retired policemen who had become messengers at the Yard, came in, holding a tray with great care. Lunch! Gideon had forgotten that he had told Tiger to send for some. The man walked past the desk with a nod and a smile at Gideon, placed the tray on a small table by the side of the window, straightened out and beamed in self-congratulation.

"Haven't spilt a drop, sir!"

"Good. What have you brought me?"

"Green pea soup, sausages and mash, coffee in a pot, cream, baked jam roll, butter and cheese. You won't starve, sir."

"Better not tell my wife how you feed me," Gideon said. "She can't understand why I'm putting on weight." He sat watching as the man spread first a white cloth and then the silverware, and finally the food. He stood back to admire his handiwork and then backed away.

"Just give a ring when you're finished, sir."

"Thanks, Tom."

Gideon moved over to the table and began to eat, slowly at first, and then more heartily. Before he had finished the soup, Tiger came in with the message typed, letter perfect. Gideon altered only a word or two here and there, and added at the top: *For General Release*, then handed it to Tiger.

"Get it out in record time," he ordered.

He had nearly finished the meal when it occurred to him that he had forgotten the escaped prisoner, what was his name? Dalby, Arthur Dalby. Had there been any news of him Tiger would surely have said so.

So one of the two prisoners, rapist and murderer, had been at large for twenty-four hours.

9

AFTERNOON

ARTHUR DALBY, known at Dellbank Prison as Pretty Face, was driving along a busy road on the outskirts of London when he saw the girl, her hand raised in silent request for a lift into London. His heart leapt. She wore shorts and a kind of scarf blouse which covered her bosom but left her back bare down to the waist. These things he took in at a glance as he began to slow down.

He had chosen to come along less busy roads than the M1 and the A1 for he guessed that the police had barricaded the main thoroughfares and were checking all cars. In this north London suburb the chances of being seen were very small. His car, stolen from a car park, was one of a popular model, too usual to be noticed, and he had taken it from a place where All Day Parking was written, so that its owner was not likely to miss it until the evening.

He felt good.

Everything had gone right for him since the break, whereas poor old George Pitton had run into a search party in a matter of hours. He had read of it in a discarded newspaper, but he would have guessed it anyhow. No mind, that was the trouble with George Pitton. Thought he knew everything and actually knew practically nothing. He hadn't known, for instance, that his good pal Arthur Dalby had stashed away a couple of hundred quid in the side of a disused well, so that now he was flush. The first thing he had done, had been to buy a wig. It made him look very different from the prison-cropped creature whose picture had been shown in the papers and on television. The second thing he had bought was a suit from a second-hand shop, with big pockets, a flared jacket and bell bottom pants. Just the thing! He could hardly recognise himself, and no one else was likely to.

Now this girl was flagging him down.

He deliberately passed her, although going slowly, and then pulled into the side of the road. Traffic swished by in two busy lanes and dozens of people were on the pavement. He wanted to see her run! Here she came. Oh, boy, what a pair! And he didn't need any telling that they weren't acquainted with a bra. She swayed from side to side and he wondered what she would look like, when running, from behind. Well, he couldn't find out now. He leaned across as she bent down to look in at the window. Don't be in too much of a hurry, that was his motto! He opened the window slowly.

"Hallo, sweetie," he said.

"Room for a little one?" she asked; and flashed a smile.

She wasn't a beauty, no one could call her that. But she had pretty eyes and pouty lips and dimples. Nice. Plump and round. He pushed down the handle and she opened the door and slid in. *Gee-ess-o-phat!* Without appearing to do so he looked at her legs – and swallowed. He hadn't seen a girl for over a year, let alone touched one. But he had to be careful; if he let his hand stray too soon she might get scared, and there were plenty of traffic lights along here and she could get out whenever she wanted.

Timing, boy; timing, that was what mattered.

It was a small car. Sitting side by side they had to touch, and he noticed with glee that she did not attempt to draw away.

The last one—

He drew in a breath too quickly and the girl glanced at him.

"Where are you going?" she asked.

"Where the wind takes me, my dear," he replied.

She raised her eyebrows. "One of the funny ones, are you?"

"My very worst enemy never said I had no sense of humour," Dalby assured her, earnestly.

"Did your worst enemy ever tell you not to look where you're going?" she asked. "There's a red light in front of you."

He brought the car smoothly to a standstill.

"I will say your reflexes are good," she declared. "And you're certainly smooth."

"The smoothest ever," Dalby said, pleased.

"Where is the wind going to take you today?" she asked.

"Where do you want to go?"

"Wimbledon," she suggested.

"I don't see your racquet anywhere."

The girl actually laughed, and as he moved the car on again, she murmured: "You're cool, man, cool. Not bad at all."

He shot her a sidelong glance and pursed his lips. They were thin but well-shaped lips and very pink.

"Why Wimbledon?"

"For the bread," she said.

"You mean the dough?" he demanded.

"That's right."

He drove on for a few moments, pretending to be preoccupied with thickening traffic, actually trying to make this girl out. She wasn't ordinary. She had a "posh" voice, but it could be put on. And she talked of "bread" meaning that she was going to collect money from someone in Wimbledon. Was she going to do a job? It was on the tip of his tongue to ask her when caution interposed; she might be hitchhiking, but that didn't mean she was one of "them", the natural breakers of the law.

"Who are you going to collect from?" he compromised at last.

"My father," she answered.

"You mean he lives in Wimbledon."

"It's actually sinking in," she said, half-laughing. "I go there now and again, when I'm skint, and he always lets me have some. Enough," she added, and laughed again. "I don't spend much."

He settled back in his seat. "Do you have to be there at any given time?"

"No."

"Expected?"

"Sooner or later."

"Well, now, isn't that lucky," he said easily. "I've a little job to do on the way – a car deal," he added. "This one's giving me too much trouble and I've got a pal who will give me a square deal on an exchange. After I've done the deal I'll take you to Wimbledon, and after that we do the town, hey?"

"So long as you don't mean Wimbledon Common," she said.

He stared at her, and then roared with laughter. She really did amuse him, he couldn't remember anyone who had made him laugh so much in years. Cute, that was the word. A Cutey. And did she know the odds! 'So long as you don't mean Wimbledon Common!' What a hoot! Wimbledon Common was the cheapest place anywhere for a lay – grass or bracken, plenty of bushes, no one nosing about too much. But that wasn't for her. What could she mean except that she rated herself good enough for a bed?

He nearly brought his hand down on her leg, but he knew that if he did, it would waken something in him; lust, desire, he knew the words for it. He knew that if he could keep his hands off that warm flesh he would be all right, and that it was only a matter of waiting.

And if she led him up the garden, like that last one—

Well, she'd better look out, that's all.

Would she fight like that last one had? Fight until he had been forced to stop her screaming by pressing his hand against her throat, tighter and tighter, until she went limp.

But this one was all right. She knew her way about.

She asked, as they turned off the main road: "Where am I going to be while you fix your car deal?"

"You can come and wait," he said, "or—"

70

"I don't want to wait about in a smelly old garage," she said, and in one way he was greatly relieved; he had made the offer simply because he did not want to lose her. Not to worry! "I'm going to do some window-shopping and then have tea," she said. "How about waiting for me here in two hours?"

In two hours, it would be a quarter to six; rush hour.

In two hours, he could get his exchange done and have a car which a million policemen wouldn't notice! And "here" was a little side street near a red light, an easy place to drop her and an easy place to pick her up. He pulled into it, and then for the first time put a hand on her leg. It was as if fire ran through him; not just through his fingers and his arm but through his whole body.

"You'll be here, won't you?" he demanded, hoarsely.

"I'll be here," she said, and opening the door slipped out with a supple movement of those lovely, sun-tanned legs. She walked past a new store which displayed a banner in crimson and black letters:

THE BEST BUY IN LONDON

But she did not go in; her interest was in the smaller shops, the salons, the hairdressers, the boutiques, although she spurned everything they sold.

About the same time, on the other side of London, in Clapham, another girl of about the same age was looking at herself in a long mirror. What having a baby could do to you! But at least it hadn't changed her legs. They looked exactly the same. No one could deny that she had the most beautiful legs! Not even she, Sylvia Russell!

She laughed; then frowned.

Were they strong enough to take her to the shops?

She ought to go, for the larder was very bare and it wasn't fair to leave all the shopping for Bobby to do at the weekends. And she couldn't honestly say that her legs ached. She felt clumsy in movement, that was all, and although Bobby chided her gently, while many of her friends scoffed, she was self-conscious about her condition. Gibes such as: "Come on old girl, don't be prissy, everyone knows where babies come from," didn't hurt her a bit; but nor did they encourage her.

"We *must* have something for supper," she said aloud, and made her decision on the instant.

She and Bobby lived on the second floor of a house in a street which was due for demolition. Some houses were already down, others were empty shells. A few of the sites had been turned into car parks, others into unofficial junk yards. Their tiny flat was self-contained, and had its own separate side entrance through a door in a brick wall. This wall stretched the whole length of the house to the street, which in turn led to the High Street and a main shopping centre. She had to walk along a kind of alley between the wall and a thin wooden fence surrounding a rough and ready car park, and as she closed the side door – her private door – she saw a man standing by a vivid scarlet sports car. She thought, idly, just the job for Bobby, and walked into the street.

As she walked, the man watched her.

10

DAY'S WORK

SHE had a sense that she was being watched when she reached the street, but when she glanced round no one was in sight. She was dreaming it up! She saw two youths on the other side of the road, brightly dressed in coloured shirts and patched trousers. A few months ago these two would have whistled across at her, or called her over, even crossed the road to intercept her. They would have meant no harm and in fact it was a great compliment to her: to her figure and her appearance at all events. Now, they glanced covertly at her and did not call or wave.

Would the baby be worth it?

Oh, not just the giving up of a flippant, passing admiration, but the giving up of freedom, of being herself. She had always, even as a child, been free to do what she liked within well-defined limits which had been extended year by year. Even when she had grown old, become sixteen, begun to go out with boys on their own and not in groups, begun to understand the mystic awareness that made one boy's touch welcome and another's repellent, she had made no secret of it; even when her mother and father had found her reading an esoteric book on *Human Sexual Appetites*, it had not occurred to her to slip the book out of sight.

"Sylvia," her mother had said, quietly, "we think—your

father and I think that you are old enough to set your own standards of moral and sexual behaviour. Do you think so?"

Taken aback, she had said: "I—I think so, yes. Yes, I'm sure." Her father had said drily: "But are you sure we'll agree?"

"I don't know," Sylvia had said, and then caught her breath as she asked: "*Must* you? Should you? Haven't you always taught me that each of us is a separate individual with our own rights, our own responsibilities, our—our own independence?" She could remember how she blurted the questions out, and how her cheeks had flushed in a kind of defiance she had never felt towards them before.

"That's what we've tried to teach you," her mother had said. "Have you learned it, Sylvia?"

"I—I think so. But why ask me now. Why *now?*"

"Because in a few days' time you'll be eighteen," her father had said, "and because soon afterwards I want to take your mother away from London, out of England." After a pause, he had added: "To Australia, in fact."

"You—" She held her breath until when she spoke the words were gasps, forced from her. "You mean you're going to emigrate? Leave *England*? For good."

"We think for good," her father said, "but we can't be sure. Do you feel that you can really fend for yourself in England, or would you rather come with us?"

Leave England? London? Friends, the art school, life as she knew it, life as she loved it? No, no, no, no! And what had passed through her mind must have shown on her face, for they both burst out laughing. Soon afterwards they began to talk and plan and she found herself sharing in their excitement and understanding that they wanted new lives for themselves, that they had made sure she did not feel under any compulsion to go with them. They had put aside a little money for her, she had a job and her skills. So she had gone into the future, by herself, with the same breathless enthusiasm they were showing.

And she had loved every minute of it, and in loving, and in

74

living, the advice and teaching of her parents over the years often became as vivid as when it had first been uttered.

"You don't have to be conventional, but you still live in a conventional world."

"You don't have to conform but unless you do in a lot of ways life will be very uncomfortable."

"Better to know a dozen men and reject them later than to marry the first and regret *that* later."

"Make your own rules of behaviour but don't try to force them on others."

"If you have serious doubts about anything, cut it out."

All these, and so many others.

And every moment of living and loving and taking and giving had been joyous, for joy was part of her. Yet she had not known true ecstasy, of the body or of the heart or the mind, until she had met Bobbie. She had felt as if a knife thrust had cut into her when she had first seen him, with his curly hair and deep brown eyes, and the way his lips curved at the corners. From that moment on there had been no man for her but Bobbie, and no woman for Bobbie but her. It had been like living in another person; sharing absolutely.

And then the decision to have a baby.

At first, an abounding excitement, followed by the inevitable discomforts, which did not matter, and the limitation of freedom, which did. Can't eat this, can't drink that, can't go there, can't be every moment with Bobbie, can't swim, bathe, play tennis, run, dance.

Would it be worth it?

Yes, she told herself fiercely, as she had time and time again.

But there remained a nagging doubt.

No one whom she knew was able to reassure her absolutely. Some doted on their children, some accepted them dutifully, some—well, to some they were almost a burden. She did not understand the reasons and could not be sure how she would feel; that in itself was disturbing.

For the first time since they had left her, she wanted her

mother and her father; Bobbie, dear, darling, rather scared Bobbie, wasn't enough support by himself. Was that why she had doubts? Did she fear that the baby, stirring now, would bring about a change in their relationship? Were there already signs that his eye roved, causes for jealousy?

There was never cause for jealousy.

At the shops, she hesitated. A new Quickturn store had opened recently but in spite of its name the "turn round" at the cash desks could be terribly slow, and she didn't feel like standing.

On the other hand, even on a pound's worth of goods she would save a few pence, and saving was saving. The stirring within her seemed a gesture of agreement.

She turned beneath the huge banner with its:

THE BEST BUY IN LONDON

fluttering in the wind. She bought milk, eggs, cream and butter, biscuits and other groceries which would not weigh too heavily, and started back from the shops. It was not a long walk to the house, but her back ached already. She was not halfway home before the bag seemed to weigh a ton, and she knew she had been foolish to get so much. That was the trouble, she was held back from doing so many of the normal things.

At last, she reached the house.

There was still the walk between the wall and the car park, but that was not so bad. There was a coping on which she could sit for a few minutes, and rest. Her legs began to cramp and the child inside her kicked as if in some kind of protest, but that only made her smile.

Then she became aware of men in the car park; not one or two but several men, including policemen. She wondered what they were doing, and twisted round on the coping to watch. There were six or seven in all, and more were coming from the road at the other side of the car park. Goodness! They were surrounding the red sports car which she had noticed before, where a man had been standing. Shifting her position a few feet, she could see one man open the driving door; she thought he had a handkerchief in his hand. Another, smaller man slid into the car. In the rush of excitement she forgot her aching back, and it was a very much livelier kick than usual which reminded her that she should go home and rest: excitement, the doctors and nurses at the clinic said, was not good for her.

For the first time she felt a wave of happiness, of positiveness that she would love the child. She was absolutely sure that everything would be all right, that the child would be the making, not the breaking, of her marriage. She picked up the shopping bag, and found it surprisingly light: as light as her heart! The old gaiety flooded over her, wonderful, ecstatic, delirious! as she opened the side door with her key.

Or at least, she put the key into the lock. There was something the matter, for it did not turn, but under slight pressure the door moved an inch or two, so the lock trouble couldn't be serious. She pushed the door wider open. The bag was heavier now and heavier still as she walked up the stairs, such easy stairs when they had come here to live, so steep and difficult now. But it was only a few steps to a landing and a doorway leading to her own apartment.

She reached the landing, and then heard a sound which made her jump and started her heart beating fast in alarm.

"Who's that?" she called in a shrill voice.

There was no answer, but she looked at another door on the landing, a cupboard where she kept brooms and mops, her ironing board and other things for which there was no room in the flat itself.

Was the door moving?

She took out her keys again and thrust the front door key into the lock; this went smoothly. She turned and pushed the door, picked up the shopping bag, and rushed forward. She hadn't seen anybody, there couldn't be any danger, and yet she felt terribly afraid. She slammed the door behind her, let the bag slip and stumbled against a table. She was leaning heavily across it, her heart hammering, when she made a fearful discovery; the door had not closed.

She had slammed it hard but it had not closed.

Very slowly she straightened up, as slowly and in great fear she turned her head: and she saw the man in the doorway.

She recognised him at once; he was the man from the red car.

She did not know anything about him for she had heard nothing of the death of Dr. Kelworthy or of this man's tragedy, but she felt dreadfully afraid.

He stood, perfectly still, in the doorway. His face was swarthy, she noted, and his eyes were over-bright. He held the door with one hand, and had the other hidden inside his coat. Her breathing came in short, sharp gasps, but she did not cry out. She hardly knew how she managed to ask: "Who are you?"

He gave no answer but stepped further into the room, and pushed the door to behind him. It did not latch and he did not seem to worry. He was small and dark and as utterly alien to her as a wild beast. She made herself say once again, through chattering teeth: "Who are you? What are you doing here?" Her mouth was so dry that she could hardly get the words out.

He said tonelessly: "My wife is dead."

"Wh-what?"

"My wife is dead. My child also."

The words went round and round inside her head like some hideous jingle.

"My wife is dead. My child also. My wife is dead my child also."

"I—I'm terribly sorry, but—"

"*You* are alive, with your child," he stated.

"Yes," she gasped. "Yes. My husband will be home at any minute now, I—I have to get his meal, I—"

As if she had never spoken he drew his hand from beneath his jacket. He moved it out slowly as if to leave her in no doubt that he was holding a knife with a thin, steel blade.

She screamed, and as she did so, he leapt forward.

A little earlier, when the first police car had reached the car park, the two youths, who had passed Sylvia Russell without taking any notice of her, sauntered up to it. No one took any notice of them. When a second car arrived and disgorged plainclothes men, the taller of the two youths with beautiful pale brown hair brushed sleekly to his shoulders, called out: "What's going on, mate?"

One of the uniformed policemen eyed him with disfavour.

"Nothing *you* have to worry about," he said curtly. "We're looking for a *man.*"

The insult, so obviously intended, appeared to pass over the youth's head, certainly it was ignored as he said: "I'd still like to know what's going on."

"Well, I'd like you to get a move on," the constable retorted sharply. "We're busy and there's a crowd gathering already. I've got too much to do to stop and talk to you."

He moved towards half-a-dozen people who were approaching from the High Street; women with children and an old man. Several more were coming from the other direction, still more were turning into the street from either end; the miracle of the quick spreading of news and the assembling of crowds was being repeated.

The youth rejoined his companion, then, dodging the police cars, they slouched towards the scarlet MG. One of the men in plainclothes glanced round and spoke to a younger man, who approached the youths.

"Can we help you?" he asked.

The youth shrugged. "Maybe we can help you. You looking for the driver of that car?"

"We are," the young plainclothes officer answered sharply.

"We know where he is," said the youth, and on the instant the young officer called out: "Sir!" The bigger plainclothes man came over, not hurrying, not dawdling.

"They say they know where the driver is, sir."

"Where?" The senior officer's voice came sharp as a pistol shot.

79

"Over there," the youth said, nodding towards the house on the other side of the car park. "He was just standing here, and then the birdie in the family way came along and he couldn't keep his eyes off her. When she'd gone he went—"

The senior man took his arm. "Tell me as we go," he urged, and in an undertone added to the young officer. "Get that house surrounded, Jones, and try not to make it too obvious." He moved with the youths, both eager now, as they threaded their way among the cars. "What was he like?"

"Dark haired chap, looked a bit foreign to me. *Murder*, is it?"

"Yes. Are you sure the woman from that house is pregnant?"

"Couldn't be more sure." The detective officer began to run towards the side door of Sylvia's house.

11

CAPTURE

THE detective's name was Shea – Detective Sergeant Daniel Shea, of the Metropolitan Force. He was a much better-than-average detective but the real breaks never came his way. He did not see this as a "break" but as an emergency, but as he ran into the road and across it he told himself that he might be making something out of nothing, that it might be the man they were after, but it may simply be an old friend, or a relative. These possibilities did not make him slacken his pace. Something in the teletype message received less than an hour before and signed by the great Gideon himself had put urgency into him. Gee-Gee would not stick his neck out like that unless he were scared. And every man on the Force who had read or been told of the message, had responded with a driving compulsion.

He reached the door, tried the handle, and pushed; it did not budge and he did not hesitate. He took a set of keys out of his pocket, one of them a skeleton key, and slipped it into the lock. It proved easy to open.

He glanced up and down the road.

Young Jones was quick, too; a police van was turning into the road and several plainclothes men from the division were walking towards him, keeping close to the brick wall of the house. He pushed the door open and stepped inside, and as he did so, without making a sound, he heard a man's voice, hoarse and menacing.

The man was on a landing at the top of a flight of narrow stairs. The door leading from the landing was open and the man was halfway through the entrance.

Shea began to creep up the stairs, keeping close to the wall where there was less likelihood of the treads creaking. He hardly dared to breathe as he debated this dilemma with himself. If he shouted and distracted the man's attention it might give the woman time to run into another room, might even give her a chance to push the man away and slam the door.

These things *might* happen.

But it might also be the one thing needed to make the man act, and act fatally.

If he could get close enough to grab the man—

He went faster; a stair creaked, but the man did not turn round. From the movement of his right arm, elbow bent, it looked as if he were taking something from his jacket. At that moment a shaft of light caught the steel of a blade and made it flash; and at that moment, the woman screamed.

Shea went up the stairs like a rocket, roaring: *"Drop that knife!"* A dozen thoughts flashed through his mind, one of them that this man was the killer of Dr. Kelworthy, who had died from a knife wound in the throat; that everything pointed to his being insane. That he held a knife and could plunge it into the woman but might swing round and use it against him, Danny Shea.

The man turned round, as if on wheels.

The knife glistened as he raised it.

Shea was two steps below the landing now, and the knife was on a level with his throat. He saw the other's eyes glittering as brightly as the knife, and then he lowered his head and hurled himself forward. He felt the knife pass through his hair, and as he fell he saw the woman, face pale as mist, raise a shopping bag and bring it down with great force on the attacker's head. Men called from below, and hearty footsteps thundered up the stairs.

And Daniel Shea knew that it was all right: he'd saved her.

He did not know what the shock might do to her, but he had saved her life from a murderer's hand.

He looked at Moreno, who was on his back, and it was funny, damned funny, for it was egg yolk that streamed down his forehead and over his face; not blood, but egg yolk!

Gideon sat back in the swivel chair with padded arms, and let all the details of the outstanding cases flow through his mind. He had told Tiger to keep all but the most urgent calls from him, without adding that he wanted time to think. Several things had happened during the afternoon, one of them irritating: Cockerill had been involved in an accident on the motorway and had been delayed. Other than cuts, and a certain amount of bruising, he had not been badly hurt; but he had been severely shaken. He was due, now, about half past six; and Gideon had wanted to be home soon after then.

He had called Scott-Marie, reported the fire at the old warehouse and his fears about its significance. The poisoned Cabinet Minister, while not yet recovered, was better than he had been, and Gideon had a feeling that so far as the Home Office was concerned, the pressure had eased. That annoyed him. The case was either important or it wasn't. The fact that a Cabinet Minister was involved should not have affected it either way. His feeling had probably reflected itself in his voice, for Scott-Marie had said: "And now he's on the road to recovery you will really get your teeth into it, won't you?"

Gideon gave a grudging laugh.

"I suppose there's something in that, sir. I won't let up at all, anyhow."

"I wouldn't expect you to," Scott-Marie said drily, and he went on in a different tone: "I think I am only just beginning to comprehend what you told me. You think this murder by fire was to prevent the fish-seller from talking, and that so far we've only seen the tip of the iceberg."

"Exactly, Gideon said. He paused, trying to get the half-formed fears and ideas in his mind into some kind of shape, then went on: "I'm waiting for Chief Inspector Cockerill, the chap I want to handle the enquiry in all its aspects. He's been injured – slightly injured – in a road accident. And I'm wondering whether it *was* an accident."

Into the silence that followed, Scott-Marie said: "I think I hope it was, George."

"So do I," Gideon said. "I'll keep you posted, sir."

Now he was going through that "accident" in his mind. He had a report from Watford, the nearest town to the actual crash. A car had overtaken Cockerill on the inside and then swung in front of him, forcing him to brake sharply and causing the car behind him to bang into the back of the police car. The cut-in car's number had been noted by the police driver; it had been an old Jaguar but moving very fast.

Gideon now wondered what Cockerill himself would have to say.

His telephone bell rang, and he hoped this would be news that the other man was here early; instead, it was *Information* with the officer in charge in a rare mood of excitement. Almost as Gideon announced himself, he declared: "We've got Moreno, sir!" A great surge of relief went through Gideon and everything else faded into the background. "Thank God for that. Where is he now?"

"On his way to Fulham HQ, sir. Apparently he was caught only just in time, out at Clapham. One of our chaps was hurt a bit, but not much."

"Good chap," Gideon said, still feeling enormous relief.

He rang off, and immediately put in a call to the division which included Clapham and several adjacent areas. He knew the superintendent there fairly well; a man named Blunt. Blunt was on the line almost immediately, and after a quick: "Hallo, Hugh," and: "Evening, Commander," Blunt went on with obvious satisfaction: "So you've heard about Moreno."

"Yes. How's our chap who was hurt?"

"He'll be all right. Nasty cut in his forehead; Moreno had got another knife from somewhere. And was your general call on the mark, George! A minute more and he would have killed the woman. If you'd like all the details—"

"I'd like a full report in the morning," Gideon interrupted. "Just the essence, now. Who was our chap?"

"Detective Sergeant Shea," Blunt answered, "and it was time he had a break, he's a damned good man. I'm going to recommend him for promotion. He took the trouble to listen to a couple of hippies, who'd seen Moreno go into a house. A very quick and tidy job, thank God."

"Give Shea my personal congratulations," Gideon said, and rang off.

Bobbie Russell leaned over his wife, who lay in bed looking pale but surprisingly untroubled, and kept on saying over and over again: "Thank God the police got here in time. Thank God."

Arthur Dalby, in an early model Jaguar obviously the worse for wear, but the best deal he could get from his friend, pulled into the arranged meeting place, then sat, very tense and still, waiting for the girl. Ah, here she was. He gazed avidly at her legs, long and lovely. My God, he thought, what a pair!

Smiling, he leaned across and opened the door, "Welcome back, girlie. What do you think of this beauty?"

She got in and looked at torn upholstery and a cracked window. "Well, it's got more leg-room, I'll say that for it," she said drily.

He shot her a swift, almost wolfish look, as he started the car, and throwing back his head laughed uproariously.

He was laughing so much, at getting the car, at getting the girl, that he did not notice the policeman on the other side of the road, who most certainly noticed him. The policeman, a youngish man, did not recognise him; did not have the vaguest suspicion of his identity; he simply knew that a man who laughed like that when at the wheel of a car wasn't really paying attention to what he was doing, and so wasn't really fit to drive. No one could throw his head back like that and rear away from the wheel and still maintain full control.

The fellow was out to impress the girl he'd just picked up, of course.

The officer, whose name was Howard, Police Constable Howard, watched as the car moved into a stream of traffic. It went smoothly enough, and the man seemed to have recovered, so it wasn't worth passing on, by walkie-talkie, to other policemen along Islington High Street and further beyond. Yet the way that head went back, the way the man's mouth had opened when he had laughed, remained a vivid picture in his mind.

While he was worrying over this, the girl next to Dalby was saying to herself: "I've got to be careful with this one. He's half crazy."

Her name was Janice; Janice Westerman. Sometimes she thought she was a little crazy, too, taking the chances she did.

Kate Gideon laid down the evening paper as the telephone bell rang. Instinctively, she knew that this was George to say that he would be late; only occasionally did that particular instinct fail her. About the family room there were oddments seldom seen here these days; at one side a half-built castle of bricks, on the other books lying face downwards, their covers bright with animal pictures; and there was a tray with spoons and nursery-rhyme plates on it: the very plates most of her own children had eaten from.

"Kate Gideon," she said into the telephone.

"Kate," said Gideon, "I hate to have to say it but I'm going to be at least an hour and a half."

"Oh, don't worry, dear," Kate said. "Priscilla's been here most of the day. She brought the children over. There's some kind of school holiday."

"So *that's* where she was!"

"Did you try to get her?" Gideon laughed. "Yes. To see if she could come over, or she could persuade you to go to her. There's one good thing," he added. "Moreno won't do any more harm."

"You've caught him!"

"He's been caught," Gideon replied, "and apparently since his arrest—" He broke off, for this was no time to talk too much, but he wanted Kate to know that he felt a kind of pity, perhaps even true compassion, for the man.

Kate said: "I don't think I've ever felt so badly about anyone outside my own family." She paused, and then went on with forced brightness: "Are you sure you'll be an hour and a half?"

"At least," he said. "More likely two. And I'd better have a snack here, so you needn't worry about food."

"I'd much rather get you a meal," she said, "unless you're famished. George – I've had a silly idea today."

"How silly?" he tried to sound flippant.

"You'll think it's absurd."

"Try me," he urged.

"Well, I've thought a lot about the soundproofed attic and the piano standing up there doing nothing but collect dust, and it seems such a waste. I *used* to play, suppose I take it up again? Shut up there the neighbours won't hear a thing." When Gideon didn't respond at once she said almost anxiously: "Are you laughing at me, George?"

"Laughing!" exploded Gideon. "That's the best idea I've heard in years!"

Gideon put down the receiver with a sigh of relief. He had meant exactly what he said. In one swoop, the sense of waste and purposelessness of the sound proofing had gone, while Kate had thought of something which might make a world of difference to her. She had played, once, but all their daughters had proved to have a musical talent so far exceeding her own that she had lost heart. If the idea of playing again really caught hold of Kate there was no telling how significant it might be:

87

the thought of moving from Harrington Street might become just a vague fancy, never to be taken seriously.

Thank God!

He heard footsteps in the passage, and then Tiger's door opened. How much more clearly sounds travelled in the evening, when most of the offices were empty and the Embankment traffic was so much lighter. He could even hear a murmur of voices, and thought: surely Cockerill. There was a tap at the communicating door and Tiger appeared.

"Chief Inspector Cockerill, sir," he announced.

"Show him in, and then you get off," Gideon said. "You look dead beat. If I need anyone I can call on the night staff."

"If you're sure."

"Quite sure."

"Thank you, sir." Tiger stood aside for Cockerill to come in. At sight of him Gideon had one of the shocks of his life, for a bandage covered Cockerill's left eye and was taped to his forehead and underneath his chin. If this was to read "superficial wounds" what the devil would he have looked like if he had been badly hurt? One side of his mouth was badly swollen and bruised, too, although it wasn't covered. His hands seemed uninjured and he walked freely enough, putting out his right hand.

"Sorry I'm late, Commander," he said.

"It looks as if we're lucky you weren't a lot later," Gideon said gruffly. "Sit down." As the other man settled, rather gingerly, into a large armchair, he went on: "The first thing I want is just an opinion, Inspector – we can settle down to the details later." He sat behind his desk, looking at Cockerill squarely. "Do you think it was an accident? Or was it an attempt to put you out of action?"

As well as he could, Cockerill smiled. Normally, he was sharp-featured and thin-faced, the skin drawn tight across his bones, but now his features looked puffy. He must have taken a real buffeting about the face.

"Ah," he said, "so you smell a rat too? I haven't breathed a

88

word, and thought it better not to do so until I'd talked to you. But this smash was deliberate. I haven't any doubt whatever. In fact if it hadn't been for my driver I think we'd have been under a lorry without any chance at all. Someone was after me, Commander, and I can only imagine it was because I had been nosing around some places in the south Midlands where I wasn't welcome." He sat back, both co☐nvinced and utterly convincing.

12

FOOD MARKET

GIDEON bent down to a cupboard in his desk and took out a syphon, a bottle of scotch, and a bottle of gin.

"Will whisky go to your head?"

"Could do," Cockerill said. "You haven't got a beer, have you?"

"Certainly, but canned, and probably warm."

"Suits me – don't care for iced drinks myself," Cockerill said.

Gideon bent down again for two tins of beer of the self-opening type, and a glass tankard. He passed these to Cockerill and mixed himself a whisky and soda, sipped, added a little more soda, and leaned back.

"Cheers," he said.

"Cheers." Cockerill drank like a man who had been wandering in the desert for days, and when he lowered his tankard he murmured apologetically: "It's these drugs they pump into you. Dry you out."

"I shouldn't be surprised," Gideon said, and after a pause, added: "So, it's big."

"I think so," replied Cockerill. "That Whitechapel fire this morning – do you think it's part of the same racket?"

"It could be," Gideon replied non-committally. "I think Firmani would say so."

Cockerill finished the tankard, and leaned back cautiously in his chair. Gideon wondered if his head was aching badly or whether the drugs had numbed him; but whatever it was, either or both, did not appear to have affected his wits.

"Then it *is* big."

"What have you discovered?" asked Gideon.

"That there are at least two lorry loads of stolen fruit and vegetables taken up on the M1 every day, and off-loaded at small wholesale markets or at the branches of big supermarkets. On the surface the buying side is legal. The buyers may know that they're getting stolen goods and the managers may be taking a cash discount on the side, but I'm not sure. I am sure about the stolen produce leaving Covent Garden and I think I know how it's done." He opened the second can of beer, pulling back the little fastener too abruptly, so that the spray spurted over his face and bandages. "I'm okay," he said as Gideon started to get up. "Haven't lost more than half a mouthful!" He went on talking as he refilled the tankard. "I've been keeping an eye on Covent Garden for some time, but you know that. At first there was a little pilfering and a few fingers in the tills, which most of the market men take in their stride. Then it got bigger and the market security chaps thought we'd better take a hand."

All of these things Gideon knew, although Hobbs had handled most of the details; and it was surprising how soon information read or passed on by word of mouth could fade. He nodded, and asked: "What was special about last night's hijacking?"

"New ground," answered Cockerill.

"I don't follow you."

"Sorry," the other man said. "I'm not as clear in the head as I might be. Well, in the past, lorries have been rented and stolen goods brought from all over the market and loaded: a crate here, sack there, string bag – the lot, so to speak. No one misses a single item, and a lot of stuff is moving all the time. Until someone gets suspicious the thieves can get away with murder, but once the security chaps know what's going on, the details can be found out fairly easily. Clear so far, sir?"

"Yes."

"Last night was quite different. A lorry filled with produce from one big merchant for delivery to an associated wholesaler in Coventry was stolen – hijacked. It wasn't missed for an hour. The driver who was to take it up on the M1 was having his dinner; he came back on time, to find it gone. Somehow the name of the firm was blotted out, probably with a quick drying spray paint, and there wasn't a trace of it until it was found in an old quarry."

"Damaged?" asked Gideon.

"Good as new."

"Then they haven't a home for stolen lorries," Gideon remarked.

"Hardest things in the world to keep under cover for long, and the easiest things to check for engine numbers and chassis numbers. I wouldn't be surprised to find someone with a fleet of smaller lorries and vans, many of which might be stolen; but the big ones – no, Commander."

"I'll take your word for it," Gideon said. "What made you stay in the Midlands so long?" Seeing a change of expression in Cockerill's one visible eye he went on hastily: "That isn't meant as a criticism, man – you must have had a good reason."

"Theft of refrigerated lorry from Smithfield," Cockerill said.

Gideon stared, thinking the answer through. Cockerill gave him very little time before going on: "I wanted to find if the meat was going to the same places."

"Ah!"

"Some of the big wholesalers have sections for fruit and veg, meat, fish, provisions and groceries or dry goods," went on Cockerill. "They supply not only the small trader but the supermarket chains – it's very involved these days. You go to a fishmonger to buy fruit and to a greengrocer to buy bacon, very often. The day of the specialist is nearly over."

Gideon said: "My wife doesn't like it."

"A lot of wives who have to save five or ten per cent like it," Cockerill replied, frankly, and then added hastily: "But this is just background, sir. I went up to Coventry and Northamptonshire and got the local chaps to watch the wholesalers who had bought some of the Covent Garden stuff, to see if they'd bought some of the frozen meat." Cockerill gave a crooked smile as he went on: "The refrigerated vehicle was found in the grounds of a big industrial estate near Coventry. It's also near a very big warehouse owned by Quickturn Supermarkets. It was empty. The meat had been unloaded into small vans – I can give you chapter and verse, Commander, they did a bloody good job up there, and these small vans carried the stuff round."

"As Jackie Baker carried the fish," Gideon said softly.

"Right on the nose, sir. We traced five vans; there might be ten or twelve in all but we traced just five. Each one sold its entire stock to one of the wholesalers who bought the Covent Garden produce."

"Good," Gideon said, showing both satisfaction and enthusiasm. "Bought?"

"Oh, yes."

"Cash?"

"Some cash, some on accounts," answered Cockerill. "As with the fruit and veg there's no way of being absolutely sure the buyers knew the meat was stolen, but it looks likely. Wouldn't you think so?"

"Probably, when I've seen the general evidence," Gideon admitted. "What did you do?"

Cockerill said: "Nothing, sir."

"Question the buyers at these wholesale places?"

"No, sir," answered Cockerill. "By the time I was sure the meat had gone to the same places, I began to smell something very big, and I thought I'd better do some thinking. And conferring, Commander! I didn't want to catch a few sprats and scare off a whole shoal of mackerel."

"You couldn't be more right," agreed Gideon. "Yet—"

"They tried to get me."

"They actually did get you," Gideon reminded him. "Do you know how you warned them?"

"No, I'm damned if I do," replied Cockerill thoughtfully. "I would have said that we kept away from trouble, always had a phoney reason for asking the questions. If you ask me—" He broke off, frowning. When he didn't continue, Gideon said: "I am asking you."

"I was afraid you would," said Cockerill, pulling down the uninjured corner of his mouth. "If you ask me, sir, they have a first-class warning system. Antennae all over the place, as it were. Spies everywhere. The harder I look at this the bigger it seems to get, and if you ask me, I boobed."

Gideon asked, quietly: "How? What more could you have done?"

"How much less should I have done?" asked Cockerill. "I think that's the question. If it is a really big operation then the people who are running it might decide to close it down for a while. A few weeks, even a month or two. If I hadn't gone back about the meat I doubt if they would have got so worried. But I did."

He shrugged, then looked at Gideon out of that one visible eye with expression of bewilderment. He was not sure of himself, not sure of Gideon's reaction. That was not all. He was looking much more tired than when he had first arrived. The injuries, added to the shock of the accident and the effect of the drugs, were taking their toll. This man needed two or three days off, at least. He also needed a strong injection of self-confidence, must not be sent away from here thinking that Gideon thought he had fallen down on the job.

"You did what anyone at the Yard would have done, knowing the circumstances," Gideon said, and added quickly: "What I can't understand is why you think you went wrong."

"Isn't it obvious, sir?"

"It's not obvious at all. You alarmed them, yes. They were alarmed about the search for Jackie Baker, but you weren't involved in that. In both cases, they were forced to show their hand." Gideon hesitated and then amended: "I don't know about forced to: the fact is they *did* show their hand. So we know we're up against something big, possibly nationwide, certainly covering London and the whole of the Midlands. We needed to know. But now that we do—" He smiled dourly, and spread his hands.

"I can't wait," Cockerill said.

"You've got to," Gideon answered. "You and I don't tell a soul that we believe your accident was a deliberate attack on you. And we don't pursue the enquiries openly for a few days. That way they should be lulled into thinking there's no need to worry."

"And that way I can take time off," Cockerill said drily.

"No use working on the job until you're fit," said Gideon. He sat back, looking into that one bright eye, and went on slowly: "Why did you mention Quickturn, Cocky?"

"Well, they were very handy, and they always *are* very handy. What's more, they've bought an interest in some wholesale grocers, butchers and fruit and veg wholesalers. They've spread wide and they've got the facilities. But I've got to admit it's no more than a guess," Cockerill added quickly.

"Intelligent guesses are always worth checking," remarked Gideon. "Who's working with you on this?"

"Detective Inspector Merriman," answered Cockerill, and put into Gideon's mind a big, heavy-jowled, heavy-paunched man who was as nearly a "typical" detective pictured by the public as there was at the Yard. A few years ago Merriman had been involved in a Flying Squad accident which had broken his left knee and left him with a stiff leg. He had asked for a job inside the Yard, and had become one of the most reliable record-keepers and organisers. He did not fit into *Records* or into *Information* but had made a niche entirely for himself.

"Doing what?" asked Gideon.

"Getting a complete picture of the men at all the main markets, and the main wholesalers, sorting out the difference between the sellers and the buyers; making graphs and generally getting everything down in black and white."

"Keep him at it," Gideon said. "Any idea how long it should take him before he's through?"

"Four or five days."

"Just about right," Gideon said, and Cockerill laughed.

The near-certain thing was that nothing could be done much more quickly where the markets were concerned, and he must know it. But the investigation into Jackie Baker's murder had to go on, intensively, with Firmani in charge. Gideon brought Cockerill up to date on that: the search for the supplier of the fire-raising material, for the man or men who had locked Baker into the warehouse before setting it on fire. This way, Cockerill would rest more easily, knowing that everything was being handled under Gideon's direct guidance and that nothing was being kept from him.

It was a little after eight o'clock when Cockerill left for home; nearly half past before Gideon had finished his notes on the report, for it would be several days before Cockerill turned in a written report. Once finished, Gideon sent for his car and drove himself home to Kate.

She was downstairs, and her eyes were glowing.

"I loved it up there!" she declared. "Who had that absurd idea of moving from Harrington Street?"

At nine o'clock, Arthur Dalby was waiting, again, for Janice. He was in the old Jaguar, parked in the street not far from the big, modern house where her father lived. He knew her as Janice, now; knew that her father was a wealthy businessman; knew that he might be on a very good thing.

In more ways than one!

As that thought struck him, he thrust his head back and roared with laughter.

This time no one noticed him.

At nine o'clock, Sylvia Russell said to her husband, in a tense voice: "Darling, I think—I think it's beginning. Please—please send for the doctor."

At nine o'clock, Dr. Kelworthy's wife sat alone in the front room of the small house they had shared and stared blankly ahead of her. The strange thing was that she could not think, except of the way she had talked to Jonathan last night. If only she hadn't, if only she hadn't!

And a little after nine o'clock the three men who were directly responsible for the murder of Jackie Baker and indirectly responsible for the attack on Chief Inspector Cockerill, were gathered together in an apartment in Knightsbridge, surrounded by luxury, and faced with ugly facts and uglier fears. But they kept these fears in the background as they faced the facts.

13

MASTER PLAN

THE shortest and tubbiest of the three men sat in the middle of three armchairs, his legs so short that he had to use a stool in order to rest his feet. He was beautifully dressed in a suede suit of pearl grey, black leather shoes of modern styling, and a dark blue tie. He had a round face and blue eyes, often merry-looking. His hair was cut short but curled a little at the temples. He was Horatio Kilfoil, the *Honourable* Horatio Kilfoil, only son of an Irish peer who had served both Ireland and England well. Lord Kilfoil served on the boards of many companies, including food importing, distributing and manufacturing companies, and was wealthy in his own right.

So was his son.

He himself did not quite understand his own motivation; there were times when he told one or both of the men now with him that it certainly wasn't the profit motive only, substantial though it was. And that was true. What he didn't say, and perhaps didn't know, was that there was a flaw in his character which made him, almost compulsively, a criminal.

The second man in the long, elegantly furnished room which overlooked Kensington Gore, was very different. He was entirely self-made, profit being his only motivation. He had started life as an assistant porter at Covent Garden Market, worked – and stolen and cheated – until he had enough money to buy his own business in the market, gone into a dozen profitable side-lines, including the buying of stolen goods of any kind. Eventually he had sold out of his business in the market and set himself up as a general food distributor and producer. From this, he had extended various ventures until he owned or controlled at least a hundred food wholesalers in the country. Still not satisfied, he had started a small chain of grocery stores or supermarkets which – because he could undercut most competition – were beginning to flourish. He was a tall, austere-looking man with a high-bridged nose, and the ambition to be taken for an English gentleman. He had even acquired a convincingly aristocratic voice which could fool most of the men with whom he dealt. His name was Black, Lancelot Black.

The third man was quite different from either of the other two. He was the accountant, a genius with figures, and a brilliant organiser. He was younger than either of the others, each of whom was in the middle-forties, and he looked younger even than his thirty-five years. There was the sharpness of a ferret about his face, the upper lip protruding slightly and the chin receding; he had pinched features and large, dark eyes which had a rare quality in eyes of such colour; they were cold. Lifeless. Yet his mind was a computer in its own special way.

He was an American of Dutch extraction, and his name was Graaf, Joseph Graaf. He dressed carelessly, having no thought of appearance, only of facts and figures.

Now he sat on Kilfoil's right, while Black sat on Kilfoil's left. Coffee and brandy was on a circular table in front of them. This was Kilfoil's home; a bachelor, he found it easier to entertain the others for business than they, who were married, found it to entertain him.

They had been watching the news on television, waiting for mention of Cockerill's "accident" or of the murder of Jackie Baker.

Neither was mentioned.

"*Scotland Yard officers this afternoon arrested Paul Moreno* . . ." they heard, the announcer going on to relate the story of the death of Kelworthy. It held no interest for them, and they harked back to their own affairs.

"Cockerill must know it was deliberate," said Graaf.

"It was an act of madness," stated Kilfoil.

"We'll get more from the newspapers in the morn—" began Black, and then he drew in his breath: "Quiet!"

"*The Ministry of Food and the police, working in close co-operation, believe they have traced the source of the outbreak of food poisoning which affected diners at many of London's best-known restaurants last night,*" the announcer stated. "*Superintendent Firmani of New Scotland Yard, in charge of the investigation, does not think there is any danger of a fresh outbreak provided all stocks of. . .*"

"I knew the police were dumb," Black said. "But *this* dumb is too much."

"They're pulling the wool over our eyes," said Graaf.

"Or they cannot find out what they want to know," declared Kilfoil. "One thing is certain, gentlemen. We must be extremely careful from now on."

"The Baker business was crazy," Graaf said in a reedy voice. "To let him go round making a few pounds a day—"

"Joe, you don't mean that," interrupted Black. "Baker and a hundred like him bring in big money, and you know it. The difference was that Baker knew that I was involved, and he had to go. The others have no idea who they're working for. The real idiocy—" He stood up and began to pace the room with long, easy strides; he was a striking looking man, particularly in comparison with the other two. "The real idiocy," he repeated, "was attacking a man from Scotland Yard."

"That was a mistake, certainly," Graaf agreed.

"The man who made the mistake mustn't live long enough to

make another," said Black, very distinctly.

"We can't go around killing people with impunity," Kilfoil protested. "A murder is a murder, Lance."

"We've killed before and we'll kill again," insisted Black, "and we won't hand ourselves out a lot of hypocritical hogwash." He looked down at Kilfoil with narrowed eyes. "We're not playing for chicken feed." When neither of the others replied he turned to Graaf and demanded: "Are we, Joe?"

"No, sir," agreed Graaf. "We're certainly not playing for chicken feed."

"We're in this for millions, and if we play it cool and if we make sure no one can betray us we can be exactly where we want to be in a year from now."

"A year and a half," Graaf amended. "All right, a year or a year and a half. That's the time it will take for us to have control of all the major food outlets in the United Kingdom. That's what we are aiming for, that's what we are going to get, and anyone who stands in our way or who makes serious mistakes has to go." He looked from one to the other. "Have you any arguments?"

"On the principle, no," Graaf replied.

"So what's your objection on the practical side?" demanded Black.

"That we cut out the small business, and that we shift from the present operation to the markets, and undersell the competition until we can buy it."

"I am in absolute agreement," Kilfoil declared.

"Oh, are you," said Black, heavily. He leaned forward to pick a cigar from a box on the table, broke the band and then pierced the end with a gold pin. "Oh, so you're both in agreement, are you?" That was a growl that denoted he was both angry and impatient with them. "Well, let me remind you of one reason why I don't agree with either of you." They waited, until he had lit the cigar and tossed the match into an empty fireplace. "Twenty to thirty million pounds," he stated, flinging the figures at them with a nonchalance he had no intention of being taken seriously. "When we started out we wanted fifty millions, now we only want twenty to thirty."

"But we have it!" cried Kilfoil. "Our shares in Quickturn and the other stores—"

"Shares and money aren't the same," Black said gently. "Tell him, Joe."

"We could raise the money on the shares," Graaf said, with a streak of stubbornness sharpening his voice.

"But we're not going to," declared Black. "Not while I'm part of this organisation, and it would look bloody funny without me. We can pick that money up in a year at the rate we're going. If we stop now, if we slacken the tempo, it will give the others time to get their breath back. They're not going to have the chance. *We're* going to hold all Quickturn stock, we're going on with a cash business, and when we see a weak link in the chain, we cut it out. *That's* how it's going to be."

Graaf said slowly: "What happens if I won't go along?"

"Then you get out."

"I've got too much tied up in this to get out, and you know it."

"That's right," agreed Black. "We've all got too much tied up in this. We're going on cutting corners and dealing in cash and forcing the little shops out of business and some of the big chains, too. They close down, we buy or we swallow them up for cash – and we get the cash the way we always have. I'll run that side of the business."

"What the hell happens if the police catch up with us?"

"That will be just too bad," Black said. "But if we're careful and we don't do crazy things like attacking senior detectives they won't catch up with us. It won't occur to them that the hundreds of individual hijackings are organised by one group. They'll go on chasing one at a time, and we'll make sure no one knows who he's working for. You can leave that to me. You handle the money and the figures, Joe, and you sit with your father on all those boards of directors, Horatio, and at the end of a year"—he gave a sardonic grin—"or perhaps eighteen months, we'll be just where we want to be, with all the main food distributors in our pocket. Have you ever stopped to think how much people will pay for food when they're hungry? Have you ever considered what happens to a government which tries to keep food prices down by cutting the profits?"

He paused; and then he laughed; and in a few moments he said: "We can't afford weak links like Baker, or fools like Webber in Coventry."

Neither of the others argued any more; it was as if he had beaten down their arguments by the very strength of his will and the power of his voice.

That night, the owner of the car which had nearly killed Chief Inspector Cockerill, was found dead at the wheel of the Jaguar, which had crashed into one of the bridges spanning the M1. No one else was in the car with him, and the experienced policeman who found him said that it looked as if he had fallen asleep at the wheel. The number of the Jaguar was sent to London, and the following morning Detective Inspector Merriman checked it; it was not the number of the car which had caused Cockerill's crash, so he simply made a note of the report and the number and made no request for the dead man's car to be closely examined, or brought to London. The trouble with facts is that, to see them in their true light, the viewer has to have imagination; and this was a quality to which Merriman was almost a stranger.

But facts he collected as a bright lamp collected moths; in a way his mind was as much a computer's as Joe Graaf's.

At half past eleven that night, Janice Westerman looked into her companion's eyes, and realised what she should have realised before. He was very tired. Even when she had left her father's house and returned to the car he had been dozing. She could remember now the violent start he had given when she had opened the car door, how something akin to terror had shown in his eyes in the light of the street lamp. She hadn't spoken, and nor had he. He had taken some minutes to settle down at the wheel of the car, and forgot to put the headlights on until she told him. After that he had driven well enough, and to her surprise, he had not headed for Wimbledon Common. Halfway down Putney Hill, with the closed shop windows lighted and a few people about, she had asked him suddenly: "Are you hungry?"

"Yes," he had answered, "starving."

"There's an Indian restaurant open over there – if you like Indian food."

"You'd like any kind of food, if—" he began.

She did not know what he had been going to say. "If you were as hungry as I am," would have been apt enough, but so might several things. She was puzzled by the sudden way in which he broke off and then glanced at her slyly, as if trying to see whether she had noticed anything. "Then let's go there," she said. There was plenty of parking space so late at night, and within five minutes they were eating curried chicken, with sweet chutney, coconut, sultanas, almonds, "all the fixings", the little Indian waiter had said. He *did* eat ravenously and yet not crudely; she simply could not make him out.

Now, they were near her flat, a small apartment on the third floor of an old house in Bloomsbury, not far from the London University. She saw him caught by a fierce yawn at a time when he could not take his hands off the wheel.

She wasn't sure what to do.

She had been so sure—

She had been going to get out of the car at a red traffic light, wave and run off; he would never find where she lived.

But now she felt sorry for him; and there was more than that. There was a devil in him which she recognised, having one of her own. His looks, his talk, his touch, all told her how much he wanted her but—he was too tired! If she took him up to her apartment she believed he would drop onto the bed and fall asleep. When he woke in the morning he would feel humiliated, of course, but—well, it would be his responsibility, not hers.

Should she take the risk?

He yawned again, and the car swerved. He straightened it out quickly enough, startled and a little scared. He had nearly fallen asleep at the wheel!

"Take the first right and the second left to Mount Square," she instructed. "You'll be able to park there, and it's only a step from my place."

He parked with great care in the small square. She took his arm and half-pushed, half-led him to the house where she had her flat; twice he actually stumbled on the stairs. Once inside he stood and looked about him, stupidly. She led him to the bedroom, and he dropped onto the bed, yawning widely.

She pointed to the bathroom, then went on to the big living-room where she had a day bed on which she proposed to sleep. She waited for ten minutes or so and then peeped into the bedroom. He lay, inert, shoes on, tie on, fully dressed. He did not notice her unlace his shoes and pull them off, or unfasten his tie. It was while doing this that she noticed something strange about his hair; a moment later it dawned on her that he wore a wig.

She locked him in before she went to bed.

He puzzled her, but she was also intrigued.

14

MEAT MARKET

NEXT morning, the newspapers chose the murder of Kelworthy and the capture of Moreno as their main theme. All three of the men who had met in Kilfoil's flat searched for and found mention of the murder at the warehouse and the poisoned food, but neither was given much space. The *Globe* ran a main inside feature on prison escapes, finishing with the latest one and the fact that Arthur Dalby was still at large.

In the *Stop Press* of three newspapers was a single sentence, which read:

Mrs. Robert Russell who was yesterday attacked by Moreno, currently charged with the murder of Dr. Kelworthy, gave birth to a baby girl in South West London Hospital last night.

Kate read this out to Gideon when, for once, the newspapers arrived before he left for the office. Detective Sergeant Shea, still glowing from the message from the Commander, read it with deep satisfaction. The two long-haired youths who had done as much as anybody to save the woman, read it with a kind of embarrassed satisfaction.

Police Constable Howard read it, also.

That was when he was having his breakfast in the front room of a small guest house not far from the local police headquarters. Then he saw a Jaguar pass, fairly new and wine red, not like the battered black one he had seen yesterday evening, but the combination of events reminded him of the way the driver had thrown back his head and laughed. Why should such a simple thing affect him so? He told himself there was a vague familiarity about the driver's face but he could not place the man who was etched so vividly on his mind's eye.

Within ten minutes of going on duty he was within sight of an accident in which a youth at the wheel of a battered-looking Volkswagen crashed into a Ford, crumpling the driving door, and seriously injuring the driver. PC Howard gave no more thought to the man who had laughed. Here was a serious job to do; an ambulance to summon, traffic to control, a hysterical passenger to calm, people to hold back from a determined endeavour to look at the driver of the Ford, who was bleeding freely.

What made people such ghouls?

Gideon talked with half-a-dozen superintendents at briefing sessions that morning, including Firmani, who had a fully detailed report on his previous day's work. No one had yet discovered where the incendiary material had come from; no one appeared to have seen the start of the fire.

"Most of it's routine, now," he remarked.

"Yes," Gideon admitted, "but finding all the other van salesmen who call on restaurants isn't, and I don't want any of them alarmed."

"Discretion is my middle name," Firmani assured him, and went bounding out of the office.

Merriman, summoned for the first time to the Commander's office, showed the gradual accumulation of facts and figures, and a total of theft value that startled Gid"Over eleven million pounds-worth! Is that figure reliable, Inspector?"

"That's just for London," Merriman assured him gloomily.

No man could have been more inappropriately named. "It will be double or treble throughout the country, sir."

"Are you getting the other figures in?"

"Yes, sir," Merriman said stolidly. "I'll have a report ready as soon as possible."

When he had gone, Gideon studied the copy of the report again, frowned, and then called the Confederation of British Industries. Could they help him to find some facts and sales figures of foodstuffs in London – at the major markets, for instance, as well as in the main shopping areas, central suburban and provincial?

"I am sure you will find that the Association of Master Food Suppliers will be able to help you more than I," the secretary of the CBI replied. "If I were you, sir, I would ask for Sir Bernard Dalyrymple."

"The head of Serveright Stores?" asked Gideon.

"That's the man, Commander. He is this year's president of MFS, and spends a great deal of time at their offices. If he's not there, they'll tell you where to find him."

Sir Bernard Dalyrymple was at the offices of the Association of Master Food Suppliers, in the Strand. He was gentle-voiced and forthright in manner.

"I hope you will soon be able to tell me why you need these figures, Mr. Gideon, but meanwhile—yes, I am sure I can get some by mid-afternoon. Will that be in time?"

"Splendid," Gideon answered appreciatively.

"May I ask now why you're interested, Commander?"

"We've had so many thefts lately I'd like to get a proportion of goods stolen as against general turnover," Gideon told him. "It may prove to be very illuminating, or it may be so negligible as not to matter."

"I don't think you'll find it negligible," the other man said. "There's one *very* interesting thing which I'm sure has struck you, Commander. I don't know whether we would have thought much about it if one of your men – Mr. Cockerill, would it be?"

"Probably."

"Well, someone with a name rather like that raised the question and we prepared some tentative figures. The point is that although food may be stolen it's nearly always sold. It isn't a loss in actual food, it's simply a loss to the producers or distributors from whom it's stolen. I would say it is a very substantial proportion," Dalyrymple went on.

"Such as?" Gideon asked.

"Four or five per cent."

"My God!" exclaimed Gideon. "That's a lot of money!"

"It is indeed," the President said, "and whichever of my hats I am wearing I am keenly alive to it. Er—I don't know whether it would interest you, my deputy has an appointment at Smithfield this afternoon at three o'clock. The market won't be very busy at that time, but one of the Chief Security Officers and the Public Relations Officer are going to prepare some figures for me. I'd rather thought Mr. Cockerill would be there."

"He's off sick," Gideon explained. "But I would very much like to be."

"Three o'clock then, at the main entrance," the other said.

Gideon rang off, but was soon talking to the secretary of another group, the Food Retailers Association, who said in a worried voice: "There's so much savage price-cutting a fantastic number of our smaller members are being forced out of business. Some of the smaller chains are feeling the pinch, too. There isn't much doubt what's causing it," he added bitterly. "The big boys mean to squeeze and squeeze until there's no room at all for anyone else. But I'll gladly send you details of bankruptcies and losses, Commander."

When Gideon rang off, he held the instrument under his hand for much longer than usual.

Janice Westerman was wakened by the telephone bell. It appeared to be muffled. She could not understand it, until she turned over in bed to look at the instrument and saw a hand covering it.

It was her "guest's" hand, and he was standing by the side of her bed staring down at her. He was wearing an old towelling dressing-gown which she had had for years; it was short enough to show his legs, bare and hairless. His wig was on straight again.

She remembered with a pang of fear that she had locked his door last night.

"Move over," he said.

She began to rise on one elbow. She wore a shift type nightdress which draped loosely over her full bosom; it had no sleeves, and was cut in a shallow curve at the neck.

"How did you get out?"

"No one locks me in, sweetie," he stated. There was a peculiar smile on his thin lips, which had a frightening effect on her. "No one, ever, anywhere, locks me in. You'd better get that straight."

"I must go—" she began.

"You aren't going anywhere," he said in a taut voice. "Move over." When she stayed on her elbow, her heart palpitating, he lurched forward with devastating suddenness. With one hand he gripped and then ripped the neck of the nightdress, with the other he thrust her across the bed. She had never known such violence, seldom violence at all, and her fears were near screaming pitch. He ripped the nightdress down to the bottom hem, and then flung the dressing-gown off himself.

"Now," he said, close beside her, "you do what I say. Just what I say. That way you aren't going to get hurt."

She was trembling from head to foot, but there was enough detachment in her to realise that it would be better not to struggle.

She was fairly experienced in a rather shoddy way, but this man's excesses amazed her.

She thought: He's been starved of sex for years—

"Now, beautiful," he said, between gasps, "you and me can get along all right if you just remember who's master here. Just do what you're told, see – and you'll find it works out the same every time: you'll find yourself joining in!" He gave her a squeeze which almost drove the breath out of her body, and then went on: "Now I'll have a cuppa, and breakfast in bed." Quite suddenly his whole body seemed convulsed with laughter. "I haven't had breakfast in bed for a long time, sugar plum. Make it extra-special!"

Gideon stepped out of his car a few minutes before three o'clock that afternoon, and looked about him. Standing by another car was Greerson of the City of London Police, for Smithfield was also within the City boundaries. They shook hands as a third car drew up and an extremely tall man in a clerical grey suit and a bowler hat got out of the back seat; he seemed almost to unfold himself, and when at his full height was at least four inches taller than Gideon, who seldom had to look up at any man.

"Commander?" It was the pleasant voice of the deputy president of the Association of Master Food Distributors. "I am Reginald Appleby." There was a little flurry of introductions and handshakes.

"I've brought Miss Pearson because she has all the facts and figures at her fingertips which is a lot more than I have. You don't mind a photographer, do you?" Another man was hovering in the background, a man with a big head and a thin neck, manipulating a huge camera into position.

"I don't mind what photographs are taken," Gideon said, "but they mustn't be used until we give the OK."

"My word on it," said the deputy president. "Now, where would you like to begin?"

"If you were going to steal a refrigerated lorry load of meat, how would *you* begin?" asked Gideon. "I'd like to see how the deliveries arrive, where they're kept, how they're loaded."

Gideon felt chilled from the refrigeration. Surprised at the hugeness of the stocks, he wondered what this place would be like early in the morning, when the market was at its busiest.

"That's the time when big lorries could come in and be loaded up with meat and taken off without much trouble," the deputy president said, "but if you ask me, Commander, a lot more is likely to go from the docks, when the ships come in and are unloaded from New Zealand and the Argentine."

"And Australia," piped up Miss Pearson.

"And Australia, of course. A driver and his mate could get away with a lot that way, once the unloading started. Often have ten or twenty at the quayside, don't they, Miss Pearson?"

"From New Zealand, the Argentine *and* Australia," she declared. "And some from Europe, particularly pork from Denmark, but some comes in from Poland and Czechoslovakia and West Germany, *and* France," she added. "And only a proportion of it comes here these days, Commander. More here than any one place, of course, but there is a great deal that goes direct from the docks to provincial markets. Some of the big chain stores have two or three lorry loads at a time which start off from the docks and call at their biggest stores to make deliveries." She was a small, grey-haired woman, with an over-exposed, projecting forehead. She wore ugly, unbecoming clothes, but to Gideon she stood out amongst these people, not simply as a personality, but because her heart was so obviously in her job. She added crisply: "There's a ship from New Zealand just beginning to unload. We'll be getting part of a load here tonight but the provincial deliveries will start almost at once. I happen to know that the ship's been cleared," she added, with a positive little nod. "And I can easily arrange it."

Gideon thought: Why not let her, while she's in the mood? And if she arranges it, there won't be so much fuss as if we arrange it ourselves.

But there was protocol: first, a word by telephone with the Divisional Headquarters to say he would be there. Next, a word with the Port of London Authority Police, to make sure no toes were trodden on, because officially they were the autonomous security authority within the docks; next again, a word with the particular branch of customs which cleared cargoes and ships before they could be unloaded.

No: he mustn't go. His presence would attract more attention than he wanted.

"I wish I could," he said regretfully. "Another time I hope. Taken by and large you think that the big containers and big deliveries could more easily be stolen or side-tracked from the docks than from here?"

"Far more easily," she said, with a sharp glance at the deputy president. "I've always said our security could be tighter."

"But once you make the security too tight you look as if you suspect the porters of theft and get trouble that way," said the deputy president ruefully. "It's a difficult world, Commander. Every job has its own problems. But that's an internal one."

"It's not simply internal if it involves the theft of food," Gideon said, and for the first time Miss Pearson smiled. He wondered what she would look like without her spectacles. Certainly he had said what she had wanted him to say; as certainly he was greatly in her favour when she dispensed tea and cream cakes before the party left.

15

CHANCE

"MERRIMAN," Gideon said next morning, when the big and stolid Detective Inspector was in his office, "have you taken into account the amount of direct theft from the docks, before the goods reach the markets?"

"Oh, yes, sir," answered Merriman. "It's a pretty big proportion, but I haven't got the exact figures yet."

"Substantial?"

"Very, sir."

Gideon nodded. "Have you heard how Mr. Cockerill is this morning?"

"Yes, sir. He telephoned some instructions."

"Oh, did he," said Gideon, stifling a laugh. "Well if you don't get on with them you'll be in trouble when he gets back."

"No fear of that, sir," the big man assured him; there did not seem to be a spark of humour in his make up. "I'll get it done."

Another man might have explained what he had been told to do, but Merriman stood silent, responding only to direct questions. And another man than Gideon might have asked those questions, but Gideon sensed this man's pride in his job, sensed too that he would be a stickler for rules and regulations: he should report to Cockerill, *Cockerill* should report to him, Gideon.

"All right, thanks," Gideon said. As soon as the door had closed on the man he rang for Tiger, who did not come in at once; did not come, in fact, until Gideon's fingers hovered over the bell-push again; but then the door opened quickly and Tiger arrived with a rush.

"Sorry, sir. I was caught on the telephone."

"That's all right," Gideon said. "How well do you know Inspector Merriman?"

"Fairly well, sir. He's very thorough."

"Yes. Check with him at least twice a day to find out if he's got anything new to report or any final figures." He did not add that he thought Merriman might hold back interim reports until Cockerill came back, Cockerill almost certainly knew how to handle him. "Anything very exciting in this morning?"

"Well—one thing could be, sir," said Tiger. "It's a report. . ."

Police Constable Howard was worried.

It was not often that a single mind-picture stayed with him as long as the picture of that driver of a battered Jaguar with his head thrown back and his hands momentarily off the wheel, but it was as vivid this morning as ever it could be. He was at the Divisional Headquarters, making out a report on the accident between the Volkswagen and the Ford. That case was going to give him a lot of trouble, he knew, because the Ford driver had died, and all kinds of development might follow. Certainly there would have to be a check on careless driving; so they would need witnesses for that, and witnesses had a habit of vanishing into thin air. Then there would be the Coroner's inquest, a special report was needed for the Coroner. And the insurance people were already asking questions, and if the dead man had been heavily insured then the insurance people would check everything, especially possible negligence on the part of the dead driver, so as to cut down the size of any award for damages.

This case, PC Howard knew, might go on for years before it was settled.

He put the report aside, about eleven o'clock, and went to the canteen for a cup of coffee; he was allowed a break of twenty minutes. For some reason the canteen was crowded this morning and he sat down at a table at which three other policemen, one a sergeant, were sitting. The sergeant, senior in age, as well as in rank, was listening to a boyish-looking constable, who was saying: "I only just wondered, sergeant. I know London's the last place I'd come to if I wanted to hide."

"Maybe it is but a lot of people think they can lose themselves better in a crowd," replied the sergeant. "And whether you like it or not you've got to find a way of picking out a familiar face—"

"Don't you mean a face that *ought* to be familiar?" demanded the second police constable.

The sergeant put his head on one side and looked as if he were going to deliver a blockbuster to the young chap who had both interrupted and corrected him. Instead, he nodded slowly and admitted:

"Yes, that's what I do mean. How many of you would *really* pick Arthur Dalby out of a crowd," he went on, and before any of the others could reply he continued: "if he wore a wig, for instance, or a beard; or if he changed his colouring, or put false heels in his shoes or padded his clothes." Now the others were silent. "You've got to know everything about a man and learn it off by heart, and don't tell me you can't – if you can't you'll be a copper all your life, you want to see the way the CID works. You've got to study the man. For instance, there's a piece in the special sheet sent round with the *Police Gazette* this morning. Have you all read it?"

One of the men said: "I looked through it. Description of Arthur Dalby, isn't it?"

"Isn't it," jeered the sergeant. "You ought to know."

"Well, the others haven't even read it yet," the man protested.

"Well, you make sure you read it and study it *and* commit it to memory. Dalby's got a smaller left little finger than usual, that's one thing I didn't know. And when he grips the wheel of a car, he spreads his fingers out, that's another. And he's got a laugh like a hyena, when he laughs he—"

"My *God,*" breathed Howard. "It was Dalby!"

The words came out with such a blast that they silenced the others absolutely; and then he stretched across and without a by-your-leave took the sheet from the sergeant's place and stared at the profile picture of the escaped murderer. He drew in a long hissing breath, and went on as the sergeant began to speak.

"It was him. He wore a wig; and that fooled me. Changed his profile, but—he spread his fingers over the wheel and he laughed like a maniac. He was in an old Jaguar, just off Islington High Street. He . . ."

Gideon waited for a call to come through, drumming his fingers on the desk and looking at a menacing grey cloud which hung low over the river. Before him was one of the special sheets which sometimes went out about wanted men, and this was a particularly good one. The details of Dalby's mannerisms were fascinating in themselves. He turned the sheet over to see if the author of the piece was named, but there were not even initials. He called Tiger on the inter-office machine.

"Tiger, find out who did this special insertion for the PG will you?"

"Yes, sir. Good isn't it?"

"Very." Gideon heard the first warning ring of the operator's telephone and rang off. It was remarkable how one could go along with a method or a situation and think it first-class and then stumble upon an improvement. He lifted the other telephone as it began to ring full blast.

"Sharples? Hallo, Mike." Sharples was only a few years younger than he, and soon due for retirement. "Gideon . . . This report about Arthur Dalby being seen. How reliable is the chap who put in the report?"

"I would say absolutely reliable," answered Sharples, speaking with a noticeable north country accent. "I've had him in my office and questioned him for half-an-hour without shaking his story. Apparently he noticed the laugh first, and he saw the man with his fingers spread wide and off the wheel for a moment. Thought of checking that he was sober, then decided he was all right and out to impress his girl friend."

"Ah. First I've heard of a girl friend. "

"I don't mind admitting it worries me," Sharples said. "He has a reputation for stringing them along for a few days and then doing unspeakable things. He—"

"I know his reputation."

"Sorry, Commander. My chap Howard said the driver straightened up at once and was driving well enough, so he didn't follow. But he *did* get the car registration number."

"Good!"

"It was a 1958 or 1959 black Jaguar, right wing crumpled and looking the worse for wear. Licence number 8512 BD. I've checked," went on Sharples, "and that's a licence number issued in 1959 by the Northamptonshire County Council, but the records show that it's changed hands seven or eight times at least. And it may have changed again without the licensing authority being informed."

"Have you put a call out for it?"

"Thought I'd check with you first," replied Sharples. "I've only had the full details for ten minutes or so."

"I'll tell *Information* to expect details from you," Gideon said. "Which way was the car heading?"

"On a one way stretch of road towards the West End." '

"Hmm," Gideon paused for a few moments and then went on: "Well, first we want the car, then we want anyone who's seen the car. Then we want a description of the girl."

"Howard's done pretty well on that," Sharples said. "About twenty, long hair, very short hot pants-type jeans, scarf, blouse. The kind who ask for it. Howard says that on reflection he thinks they had an appointment. I'll add her description in the general call."

"Yes. And once we find that car we want a house-to-house search."

"Only hope we find it," said Sharples, in a tone which made it clear that he rather thought they wouldn't. "He could be anywhere by now—and could have dumped the car, too."

"Yes. What else are you doing?" asked Gideon.

"There are several shops, a news-stand and a café near the spot where he picked the girl up. I'm going to send Howard out with a plainclothes man to find out if anyone noticed anything." Before Gideon could comment Sharples went on: "What about issuing descriptions to the Press, TV and radio?"

"Yes, widespread," answered Gideon. "Get our Identikit people to draw full face and profile of Dalby as he would look in the kind of wig he was wearing. Better have Howard have a talk to them, they might get a good idea of what the girl looked like, too. Put Dalby on the screens and in the newspapers with and without wig."

"Right," ejaculated Sharples.

Gideon rang off, not displeased, but troubled. One of Sharples' sentences hovered in his mind: "The kind who ask for it." There wasn't a girl in the world who "asked for" the kind of treatment which Arthur Dalby was likely to mete out. At the time of his arrest and during the enquiries which had followed, he had been revealed as a sadistic pervert who seemed to get the greatest satisfaction from behaving, early in an intimate sexual association, with extra-normal virility, until suddenly something seemed to crack in his brain.

For PC William Howard it was a day of days. First, the obvious astonishment of the sergeant at coffee break; then the equally obvious approval of a man he knew only as an aloof and distant figure, the superintendent; soon a visit to the Identikit and Photography departments and Scotland Yard, where about twenty wigs had already been brought in on loan from a nearby hairdresser. Unhesitatingly he had pointed to one of the wigs, identical to that worn by the man in the car. With a few deft strokes an artist added it to the photographs of Dalby, and Howard could not conceal his excitement.

"I'm more sure than ever – that's him all right!"

He was less happy about the attempt to get a good likeness of the girl; but one could not be a hundred per cent sure on everything.

To cap the day he went with two detective officers of the CID branch to question shopkeepers and the newsboys and passers-by at the spot where he had seen the laughing man.

At half past five that afternoon, the first report came in. The battered Jaguar with the registration number 8512 BD had been found in Mount Square, near Russell Square, in Bloomsbury. Heavy rain and leaves had half-covered the car, lessening the chance of it being found hours earlier.

At ten past nine that evening in front of his coloured television set in the comfort of the living-room in his Wimbledon house, Janice Westerman's father sat alone watching the news. This had become a ritual since his wife had left him, two years before, for a man fifteen years younger than he. At heart, he was lonely, despite his material success and despite being able to afford expensive "consolations" to ease the boredom of his new bachelorhood. He knew that he was really too old to be an understanding father to Janice. He had learned that criticism and. condemnation of her way of life did nothing to help their relationship, and for the past year they had come to a working agreement: if she were in need she would come to him, and he would not ask why, or for what purpose, she needed the money. She was never greedy, and, in a strange way, he had come to enjoy these brief visits.

He heard about the Jaguar, about Arthur Dalby, and the fact that he had a girl with him. Then an Identikit picture was thrown onto the screen, and he felt a stab of recognition. The newscaster was describing her.

"Full figure, slightly plump but not fat, wearing blue jeans cut short as hot pants and fitting very tightly,

*wearing a halter or scarf-type blouse of vari-coloured
pastel shades . . ."*

Janice Westerman's father felt as if he had been turned to
stone.

16

MONDAY, TUESDAY

GIDEON heard about the call to the Wimbledon police by Mr. Westerman in the middle of the Saturday morning, when he was cleaning the lawn mower. Kate, watching him from the kitchen window, saw him frown as the telephone bell rang. He was caught between frustration at being interrupted at a job he wished to finish, and relief that he could leave it with a clear conscience for a few minutes. There was an extension in the kitchen, and after a moment Kate called: "It's *Information*, George."

Why wasn't it Tiger? Why did the Yard have weekends? Why didn't the whole staff, civil as well as uniformed and plainclothes, work in shifts so that the Yard was fully manned seven days a week? These thoughts teased through his mind as he approached the back door. Step and floor were covered with an old builder's canvas, a manoeuvre of Kate's so that neither he nor the children trampled dirt into the kitchen. The telephone was the wall type, near the door which led to the passage alongside the stairs.

"Gideon," he stated gruffly.

"Thought you should know, Commander, that the girl with Arthur Dalby has been identified. Her father saw her Identikit picture and heard her description, and called in last night.

We've checked her fingerprints, left on a cigarette box and furniture when she was at home on Thursday, with fingerprints in the car, identical, sir."

"Good. Did the father know she knew Dalby?"

"He says he doesn't know *who* she knows, sir. She lives her life away from home, he lives his. He doesn't even know her address."

"Good lord!" exclaimed Gideon.

"But we've got some good photographs," *Information* went on. "Should we use them in place of the Identikit picture?"

"Yes. Is that all?"

"Mr. Lemaitre was on the buzz – was calling for you, sir, and I told him you wouldn't be in this morning unless something special turned up."

"If he calls again, ask him to ring me here," Gideon said. "Anything else, while I'm on?"

"Nothing really special, sir," *Information* told him. "Two refrigerated provision lorries were hijacked outside a transport café last night, and one containing cigarettes was stolen from a wholesaler's warehouse. The usual crop, sir – as I say, nothing out of the ordinary."

"No," said Gideon. "Thanks."

He rang off, thinking "nothing out of the ordinary". That is exactly what he would have said a week ago, but now anything to do with food thefts was very out of the ordinary indeed. He wished he had asked what the latest figures on the ptomaine poisoning were, and then reassured himself that Firmani would keep him advised of any serious development, Saturday or no Saturday. Kate was bending down in front of the oven, and already, whatever she was cooking smelled good. A casserole – no, the lid would keep the smell in. Certainly not a roast. Perhaps one of the old-fashioned dishes which he liked too much; hot pot. He watched her as she straightened up, wondering why some people had such natural grace while others looked so clumsy doing everyday things.

"Hot pot?" he asked.

She nodded.

"Bless you. I—"

The front door bell rang, making both of them start, because they had been so absorbed in each other for those few moments. Then Gideon glanced down at his gardening shoes and Kate said: "I'll go." He looked after her, listening. The note of pleased surprise in Kate's voice could not be mistaken.

"Why, Lem! What a pleasant surprise!"

"It certainly is for me," said Superintendent Lemaitre. "If I'd come at the worst possible time you'd still pretend I was welcome. Is George in?"

"He's in the garden."

Good idea, thought Gideon, and withdrew to the garden quickly. He was lifting the grass box when Kate called out: "George, it's Lem." A moment later Lemaitre appeared beside her, looking spick and span, even slightly pernickety, in a matching shirt and tie with coloured handkerchief.

"My!" breathed Gideon. "Sartorial splendour indeed. My hand's a bit dirty, Lem."

Lemaitre turned and winked at Kate.

"Cracks every crime problem in England, but doesn't seem to have much success with his lawn mower, does he! 'Morning, George! Want some help?"

"And spoil those spotless cuffs? Kate would never forgive me."

"It's not your wife who would have to forgive you but mine. She sends her how-de-dos, by the way. Nearly brought her but she's got some charity thing on, bazaar or some such nonsense! Well, George, you'd never believe what *I've* done."

"Lem," Kate interrupted. "Will you have some coffee? Or is it time for something stronger?"

"Coffee'd be just the thing," replied Lemaitre. He picked up a trowel and began to scrape the blades as if it were second nature. Gideon sat on a bench and watched, while Kate went into the kitchen. "I checked on the quayside deliveries of the old frozen carcasses, George. Do you know what I found?"

"What do you think you found?" asked Gideon warily.

"Good old George. Never believe a thing until it's down in black and white and can be used in evidence!" He went on scraping the muck off the blades but looking occasionally at Gideon.

One thing was certain: Lemaitre would not have come right across London on a Saturday morning unless he was sure that it was a matter of extreme importance. He had a habit, his main weakness, of jumping to conclusions, but he seemed superbly confident this morning. True, he was obviously determined to impress Gideon, but if the information was significant Gideon was eager to be impressed. The only sounds were the scraping, the rattle of cups and saucers in the kitchen, and the trilling of the birds.

"All right, Lem," Gideon said when he judged the moment right. "Let's have it."

"You might or you might not believe that whole lorry loads of the frozen mutton, lamb and beef, especially from New Zealand, leave the docks but never reach their intended destination. Not one, not two, but half-a-dozen each shipment." Lemaitre finished scraping, and wiped his hands against one another fastidiously. "It's the same as the old trick of putting a railway wagon in a siding, and losing it long enough for it to be emptied by night. George, this is a *very* big job."

Gideon stared at him, his eyes narrowed.

Kate's voice drifted out from the kitchen. "Are you coming in for coffee?"

"Half a mo', Katey," Lemaitre called, and stared back at Gideon.

Gideon said gruffly: "How did it come to grow so big. How did we *let* it happen?"

"Easy," Lemaitre stated.

"I don't want any guesses, Lem."

"No guesses. It isn't from me, either, it's straight from the horse's mouth." Seeing the storm gathering on Gideon's forehead, he added quickly: "It's from Edie Pearson, the

Smithfield woman. She was over at the docks last night, and I got a call to go and looksee. That woman's got an analytical mind, George, she—"

"How did it happen?"

"One or two key men at the docks, or at a market, signing for nine lorry loads going out when there were ten. General falsification of papers – a very clever mind behind it, Edie says. A dozen drivers in the know and say a dozen others – checkers, superintendents – and that's all. That's *how* the stuff goes, George. How it goes from other big food warehouses, too – the only commodity that doesn't seem to suffer much is tea, and anything under bond. Question is – who buys it?"

"Yes," Gideon agreed. "Who buys it. We should have some idea on Monday, Merriman's collating information about wholesalers and main distributors."

"That old ox still around?"

"Let's go and have that coffee," Gideon said. "Have you told anyone else, Lem?"

"No, sir. The Commander gets to know the big stuff first, in my book."

Gideon put a hand on his arm for a moment in a rare gesture, and as they went into the kitchen, he said: "Thanks for cleaning the lawn mower."

Kate was in the living-room, hovering over the coffee percolator, tall cups, biscuits and chocolate cake. She asked Lemaitre to stay for lunch, but he refused with obvious regret. By the time he had gone it was after twelve o'clock, and Gideon was thinking more clearly than before about the situation.

It simmered in his mind all the weekend.

There were the moments of sadness, when a van collected the furniture from Mrs. Jameson's attic flat. There were minutes of deep satisfaction when both Gideon and Kate were upstairs in the soundproofed attic, Kate playing, Gideon humming, sometimes a hymn, sometimes an old music hall song. A newspaper reporter rang up to ask if Gideon had any comment about Arthur Dalby and his girl friend Janice.

"No. And you should know better than to call me at my home on a—at any time," Gideon corrected hastily.

"Have to take a chance sometimes, Commander," the reporter said reproachfully. "Did you hear about Sylvia Russell and her new baby?"

"I know she *had* a new baby."

"And both doing fine," the reporter said. "I showed her and her husband one of your special SOSs about that. If they'd had a boy instead of a girl, they'd call it George!" Before Gideon recovered from that laughing statement, the reporter went on: "Is it true there's a special investigation going on about large scale thefts from the big markets and from the docks?"

A bright young man indeed, thought Gideon; and there did not seem much doubt that this was the question he had really called about. There was no time to hesitate, and Gideon was never in favour of the direct lie.

He said: "There will be, if the thefts really reach a big scale."

"Come off it, Commander! They're enormous, and you know it!"

"What newspaper do you represent?" asked Gideon mildly.

"The *Echo*. And by the way my name is Elliott. Commander, off the record, are these food thefts worrying you?"

"All thefts worry me."

There was a moment's pause before the other said: "Well, thanks, Commander. Goodbye." He rang off before Gideon could make any further comment. Gideon waited only a few moments before lifting the receiver and then skimming through the *E* to *K* section of the London Telephone Directory for the *Echo*. He asked for the News Editor, who came on briskly: "Who's that?"

"Commander Gideon of—"

"Good-evening, Commander! How can I help you?"

"Do you have a reporter named Elliott?" asked Gideon.

"No," the man replied. "Are you planning a special news story on food hijacking?"

"I'm not, but features might be. Care to hold on?" Gideon

held for what seemed a long time but the other came back at last and said: "No, Commander. It's not on our schedule. Do you mind telling me what this is all about?"

"Someone named Elliott is using the *Echo* as a cover," Gideon said.

"Could be a freelance," observed the News Editor. "It has happened before. If we get a story offered, I'll let you know."

"Be glad if you would," Gideon said, and rang off.

He went back into the living-room, where Kate was watching the Sunday night play on a BBC channel. She was so intent, that he didn't disturb her. But in some ways he was more worried than ever.

Later that evening, Kilfoil, Black and Graaf met again in Kilfoil's apartment, sitting in their accustomed positions, drinking their accustomed drinks. But there was, now, a tension which had not been there even on the meeting earlier in the week. Obviously they were waiting for a telephone call, or for a fourth person to join them. Eventually a young man was admitted by a manservant. He lost no time, saying as the door closed: "I talked to Gideon, Lemaitre, Firmani and several divisional men. None of them gave me the direct negative, just said they were investigating the incidents one by one. But I don't believe them. I believe they're really going to move, that they've already started to see how big it is." He looked into Black's deep-set eyes and went on: "And when the police really get on the move, they're like a steamroller in action. Nothing can stop them. If you want my opinion you have to do some very quick thinking."

Lancelot Black asked Kilfoil: "How many men can put a finger on us, Horatio?"

"That's your job," Kilfoil protested. "How many do you think?"

"I know my side of it. I'm thinking of yours."

"Two," said Kilfoil, slowly. "Two and possibly three, know that we're working some racket."

"Joe?" asked Black, flatly.

"None," Graaf said. "I keep all the facts and figures that matter and all the names and personnel in my head. No one can get to us through me, but your twenty—man, that's dangerous."

Lancelot Black said: "If he's right about the police attitude, *that's* dangerous. So are Horatio's men. We need to keep a very careful watch for two or three more days, and if the police look like closing in, then—" He brought his hand down with a chopping motion. "We stop."

"That's what I wanted to hear last time," Graaf said.

"Well, you're hearing it now," retorted Black crisply. He narrowed his eyes as if lost in thought. "We can't take chances. We've got to warn everyone concerned and we've got to make *sure* they don't talk." The others exchanged glances while Kilfoil moistened his lips. Then Black's eyes opened at their widest and he said: "We'll call a meeting. We'll question each one and find out if he's had any trouble, or noticed that the police were being more active than usual. We'll meet at—" He hesitated, and then went on: "At our warehouse in Smithfield. Seven o'clock, Wednesday—no, Thursday. You tell your two or three," Black added to Kilfoil, "and bring anyone who might know what's going on."

As they went downstairs in the lift, Graaf said in his almost aggressive manner: "Do you think he knows what you're planning?"

"What *we're* planning," corrected Black, and laughed. "No, Horatio hasn't got a thinking cell in his brain. He 'thinks' I want to ask them questions."

"I know one thing," Graaf said.

"What particular thing?" demanded Lancelot Black.

"Nothing would make me go to that gang of thieves, partner. Nothing in this world."

"But Horatio won't be able to wait to get there," Black said, and he gave an explosive laugh. "And we'll be doing what the police want, won't we? Putting a stop to the hijacking!"

He laughed again.

Graaf didn't laugh; he shivered.

17

"THAT GANG OF THIEVES"

ONE of Gideon's deep preoccupations over the years had been: *why* did men from a good honest background, who earned a reasonable income, turn to theft, pilfering, the dozen-and-one forms of larceny which did so much harm to society and took up so much time of the police. At best a homespun philosopher, he knew that this was a motivation allied to that behind shop-lifting by women who were well-off by ordinary standards; stealing out of tills by shop assistants; "borrowing" by bank cashiers and others in positions of trust.

He could understand when there was an acute need of money to meet an emergency; he could understand the pressure caused by gambling debts, by overspending on hire purchase. He could even find excuses as well as reasons for many of these but—why did so many people who did not need to profit from crime seize the first opportunity, and then go on and on?

The drivers on the refrigerated lorries, for instance, were highly-paid; why did some cheat? Why did some deliberately go into transport cafés and overstay their break-time, knowing their vehicle would be gone when they went outside? It was not so much "what makes men steal" which preoccupied him as "what makes men with plenty of money in their pockets steal?"

There was, of course, no easy answer, unless the obvious one was right: that there was a brain defect in those who stole, just as there was a brain defect in men like Arthur Dalby, and others like Moreno. He accepted the fact that of a family of three brothers, say, born into the same background, given virtually the same care by parents, the same educational opportunities, all three would turn out very differently. One might be as near a saint as human beings ever were; another as near a devil; the third, neither saint nor positive sinner, could be merely a nonentity.

The simple truth was, then, that though he could not fully understand, he must accept the situation. It preoccupied him a great deal in the early days of the week which followed the first realisation of the size of the food thefts. Many of the men involved, and by his reckoning there must be at least twenty actively concerned, would be ordinary family men; happily married or not, according to the luck of the draw, probably proud of children who were proud of them. They were the people next door; the trusted neighbours, except that in the bitter experience of the police one could trust only those whom one knew for certain to be trustworthy.

Those van drivers really puzzled him.

Cockerill, who came in on the Tuesday morning with a magnificent purple, blue and black eye, half closed, and with some partly healed cuts and scratches, said helplessly: "They get a hundred quid a week when they do a full week – and they can work a full week whenever they want to. It beats me."

Sam Tollard was one of the drivers.

He was a married man with a son and a daughter. It was a happy enough home in an apartment block near the docks. At forty, he had managed to put a few thousand pounds aside, he had some sizeable endowment insurances, and as far as he knew, not an enemy in the world.

And as far as he knew, only he and the man who paid him for the jobs were aware that every now and again he delivered a full load of meat to a big buyer, was paid cash for it, and kept two hundred of the cash for his trouble. He had been doing it for so long that it almost seemed part of the legitimate side of his job. His work kept him away from home for long hours, but he had absolute trust in his wife, and she in him. No week passed when he did not take her and the kids a small present, and treat them to a flash restaurant and the pictures.

Roger Banner was also one of the drivers.

He was younger than Tollard but also married, and a good-natured man who played rather than watched cricket and football at weekends, and went shopping on Friday evenings with his wife, taking turns at pushing the pram which held his children, one-year-old twins Sarah and Martha.

Both these men, and all the others whom Graaf had called "that gang of thieves" received notices to be at the Battersea warehouse on Thursday at seven o'clock, even if it meant turning down a shift. It did not occur to any of the men to object. There were the long-distance drivers, the van salesmen, two or three tally-men – white collar workers – at the docks, an inspector of goods traffic on the railways, one or two key workers at Smithfield, Billingsgate and Covent Garden markets.

There was one other man involved, one who had worked with Lancelot Black since his early days, but had twice been jailed for robbery. He was an expert on explosives, and he was an expert at asking no questions. When Black told him to take sufficient nitro-glycerine to a certain warehouse at Smithfield, and exactly where to hide it, he obeyed. It was in position a day early: on Wednesday.

On Thursday morning this long-time friend of Lancelot Black was found dead at the foot of the stairs in the tall, condemned building where, he lived. His neck was broken, and the autopsy showed that he had been full of whisky; there was little doubt that the coroner's verdict would be one of death by misadventure.

On the Tuesday before these things happened, Gideon, Cockerill and Firmani, with Merriman sitting in as a kind of talking reference book, went over the facts as they were now known. Whatever his faults, Merriman had done a thorough, almost a brilliant job. He had the figures for the main cities in the United Kingdom as well as for London, and the total value of the stolen or misdirected food was colossal. Cockerill said: "It's five per cent of the total food bill, Commander."

"The wholesale total," Gideon said. "Yes. And how far have we got with the finding out where it goes?"

"No more than we knew before," Cockerill said. "As you instructed, Commander, we went carefully, not wanting to raise any alarm. We know of at least five wholesalers who take stolen goods of any kind and ask no questions; but they can only be a small percentage."

"Thousand," interjected Merriman, unexpectedly.

"I can tell you this," Firmani said, "one in six of the restaurants on my list have been buying from dubious markets. If they can save ten per cent they save it. If it hadn't been for those eels—" He broke off.

Gideon said: "The distributors must be very big."

Cockerill grunted, Merriman grunted, Firmani raised both eyes and then said:

"One big one or a lot of little ones."

"One big one, most likely," declared Cockerill. "To fix this with thousands of distributors would need a huge administration. Did you have any luck with the Food Retailers Association, Commander?"

"I've been promised some kind of report this afternoon," Gideon answered. "I'll let you know if it has much to say."

He nodded dismissal.

They went out very quietly. Gideon watched the door close, then moved to the window, taking up his favourite stance and watching the ever-changing scene. The weather had turned unpleasant in the last few days and the grey Thames was pocked by a million rain drops. He singled out one pleasure boat as it disappeared beneath Westminster Bridge, going perhaps as far as Richmond and Teddington Weir; then turned away.

There had been little briefing that morning; very few major problems had cropped up over the weekend, but that meant little. Crimes committed might still be discovered, crimes from murder to the comparatively trifling. He was ill at ease with himself, and quite suddenly knew what he must do. He called the Commissioner, who answered his own telephone in a voice which sounded a thousand miles away.

"What is it, George?"

"Do you have half-an-hour to spare, sir?"

"Now?" asked Scott-Marie, obviously hesitant. "I had planned—" He broke off. "Half-an-hour."

"Should be plenty," Gideon assured him.

"Then come along right away."

Scott-Marie was a tall, lean, military-looking man, good-looking in an austere way. Gideon, who had not seen him for several weeks, was startled; lines at Scott-Marie's mouth seemed deeper, as if a sculptor had been at work on him, chipping at the hard, leathered face. Now he waved a hand towards an angular-looking armchair. It looked too small for Gideon, but from experience he knew that it was not only big enough but also very comfortable. Scott-Marie had his own chair positioned so that Gideon did not have to face the window-light while looking at him. He did not speak at once, but waited.

"Two things, closely related, sir," Gideon said, aware of, and grateful for, this characteristic gesture. "We've been criminally slow getting onto the size of the food thefts. We still don't know the full extent of it, but it seems to have been brilliantly organised and I'm sure as I can be that it's big enough to have an effect on the national standard of living."

Scott-Marie, for once, was startled into saying: "Can anything

135

be as big as that?"

"I've convinced myself," Gideon stated, "and I've been trying to think how it could be done." When Scott-Marie simply nodded he went on, choosing his words with great care. "I think it could be done by forcing down prices, forcing the small trader out of business, leaving the largest share of trade in the hands of a few large chain or multiple stores who could fix prices as they wished." Still Scott-Marie was silent, and it was impossible to say whether he was agreeing or disagreeing. "The price-fixing wouldn't be our business," Gideon said, "but the steps being taken to reach the position from which it could be done are our business."

"Most certainly," Scott-Marie agreed.

"A major distributor must be involved," Gideon said, "and I'd like to start investigating them all." His lips widened in a grim smile. "And that's a tall order."

The Commissioner did not argue. "If it has to be done, it has to be done. Do whatever you think necessary."

"Thank you, sir. It may take some time but I'd like to plant a man in most of the head offices and main branches of the biggest chain stores." Gideon shifted in his chair. "Then there's another angle that really gets under my skin."

"And that is?"

"The way the van salesman for those eels was murdered. It was quick, callous and hideous, sir. The man who could order it could do anything. When I first started this investigation I wanted to keep it quiet, but that hasn't proved practicable. A lot of enquiries have been made. On Sunday I was questioned by a bogus newspaperman about our plans, so was Lemaitre, and several others. I'm afraid of another ruthless act if we get too close."

Gideon stopped.

Scott-Marie leaned forward, looking at him very intently. It was as if he were asking himself questions and then answering those questions, the main one being whether Gideon was absolutely serious. At last he said: "Are you saying that you think we should take some of the suspects into protective custody?"

"That's what I'd like to do," Gideon said, enormously glad that he had come here; this man was one of the few who would really understand what was driving him. "So I'm in a cleft stick, sir. Make some arrests and tell the organisers that we really are getting close to them; or let things go on as they are until we get a fuller and clearer picture which would lead us to the main criminals. If I choose either, and it goes wrong, it could be disastrous." When the Commissioner sat and waited, he went on heavily: "I'm not asking you to make the decision for me, sir. But before I decide one way or the other I think you should have the chance to veto either or both."

Quietly, Scott-Marie replied. "I'd like to think about it, and I've a man coming in five minutes. I'll be in touch in about two hours."

18

EITHER OR BOTH

AS Gideon was saying: "I think you should have a chance to veto either or both," to Sir Reginald Scott-Marie, one of the oldest police constables on the Metropolitan Force was looking into a room which was a curious mixture of grubbiness and glitter; of junk and valuables. It was on the top floor of Poberty's Buildings, in Whitechapel, on the fringe of Lemaitre's division. The constable, whose name had grown to suit him, was Old, commonly known in the division and among the people with whom he worked as "Old Charlie Old". Getting up four flights of narrow stairs had been an effort, but from the moment he had learned that his namesake, Charlie Larsen, had been found at the foot of the stairs with a broken neck, he had meant to come here.

Old Charlie Old had a great many attributes, loyalty, courage, tolerance, not being the least. But no one would have called him brilliant. His ideas, such as they were, were born out of experience, and what thinking he did was along the most conventional lines. Over the years that he had served here, and they were over thirty, he had come to know and accept a great many residents of the district, and, having a good memory, he knew who had been inside and for what offences; which wife would be faithful when her man was in prison and which would not; which mother needed watching, especially when in drink, for her children's sake; which mother managed miracles on a small or negligible income and kept a large family spick and span.

Old Charlie Old, then, was part of the district. Even when the great changes had been taking place in the operation of the Force, younger men were being drafted in and the older ones retired, he stayed. He did not know that this was because his superiors all knew that his knowledge of this particular part of London was invaluable. Even thieves in trouble would go to him, and many a wrong-doer, when taken away by the plainclothes men for a well-earned two or three years sentence, would plead: "Keep an eye on my old woman, Charlie." And Old Charlie Old would nod and say: "Right you are, Bob,"—or Syd, Jim, Joe, whatever the name might be. He always got the names right. No one would ever know how much his kindness cost him in hard cash, but he didn't smoke, had only an occasional glass of beer, and a wife who earned nearly as much as he did at a gown and mantle manufacturers in Shoreditch.

This morning, he had come back on duty after two days off, and heard about Charlie Larsen. The inquest hadn't as yet been held, but the facts were known by everyone, and it did not surprise Old Charlie that the other man had fallen down the stairs and broken his neck. The marvel was that he hadn't injured himself long before. Old Charlie's visit was due to something very different: curiosity. For Larsen, especially when on the way to being drunk, had often passed on what he called: "Li'l ole secrets". In fact he said very little, except that he had influential friends, and didn't have to worry about his future. Old Charlie Old had noticed – without actually asking – that he seldom bought groceries or foodstuffs from the corner shop, now glorified by the name Supermarket, or even from the bigger shops in the nearest main road. He had a secret source of supply. Whether he stole them or not Old Charlie could only guess. He didn't think so.

One thing Larsen had paid for was his whisky, from a nearby

off-licence.

He had no regular job but took odd jobs whenever it suited him. He was, for instance, a standby pall-bearer for a local undertaker, as well as a messenger for many of the shops.

Now, Old Charlie Old looked about the room.

The bed was solid with a good, fairly modern mattress. Two big electric heaters would keep the room warm when London was freezing. There was one hide armchair which looked inviting and two smaller, velvet covered ones. On the mantelpiece was a French porcelain clock which was of beautiful colouring and design; Old Charlie knew instinctively that it was very valuable. Next to it was a cheap alarm clock, a tin tea-caddy with a garish design, and a dozen dust-gathering odds and ends. On a corner table was a silver candelabrum, which looked as if it had been lovingly polished, next to a cracked ash-tray. A bottle of ink which seemed to have dried up, flanked another, cleaner ash-tray with some white pellets in it.

He picked one up and sniffed. It had a faint and distinctive smell, and yet he could not place it. A bit acid, he thought; it lingered in the nostrils. Then he spotted, among the rubbish on a table behind the door, something he had not dreamt he would find here: an old detonator.

He went close. Yes, that was a detonator, the kind they used in plastic bombs and nitro-bombs, which would explode either at a set time if it was wired to a timing device, or under a slight impact. He did not pick it up but asked the empty room: "Charlie, what have you been up to?"

He began to search more closely, in cupboards and drawers, until he found a half-full box of the detonators on top of a cupboard – out of sight until one stood on a chair.

"Strewth!" Old Charlie exclaimed. "He's been fooling me all these years."

He went out, closing and locking the door, going down the interminably long staircase, stepping over the white chalk marks with which the police had outlined the dead man's body.

He could have used his radio from here but he did not altogether trust walkie-talkies; they did the job all right, but bigtime crooks could get the wavelength and monitor the reports to and from policemen and headquarters. He walked, dropping a word here and a word there to people at their windows or doorways, until he reached a crossroads where he knew a police patrol car would appear soon. One did, in less than five minutes, and pulled up at his signal.

"Want some help, Charlie?"

"How about a lift to the station?"

"Hop in. Getting secretive in your old age, are you, Charlie?"

"Just find my legs get more tired than they used to," Old Charlie replied evasively.

He reported in person to a sergeant, the sergeant reported to an inspector; the inspector sent the sergeant and Charlie Old back to the flat for a closer look; the sergeant did not share Old Charlie's misgivings about walkie-talkies, and he reported straight back to the inspector.

"They're detonators all right, sir. And that's not all. There are some pellets of Firex about the place, the stuff the fire chaps think started the fire when Jackie Baker was killed. And tucked away under the bed are a couple of tins of gelignite, brand new – it looks as if they were stolen with that lot out of the Hi-Build yard last week."

The inspector immediately went up to see his superintendent, Lemaitre.

Lemaitre was in his office; it was his habit to keep his door open so that anyone who wanted to see him could do so. A closed door meant *Keep Out*, and no order was more effectively obeyed. Lemaitre, intently studying papers, looked up immediately.

"Sit down, Perky."

"I'm not sure I've time, sir," said the inspector, and launched into his story.

During this same period, Gideon buried himself more and

more deeply in the figures and the general situation, concentrating on the distribution to wholesalers and the retail outlets for the stolen goods.

Mr. Westerman spent those two hours sitting at his office desk, trying to concentrate on work, but unable to prevent his eyes from straying towards the photograph of Janice which looked up at him from a neatly folded newspaper. His secretary and everyone concerned with the business seemed almost as shocked as he.

Now and again, when alone, he would clench his fist and cry out in anguish: *"Where is she?"*

During those two hours, the door-to-door search being made for Arthur Dalby and Janice Westerman was slowed down by two bank robberies, two smash-and-grabs, and a suspected plot to rob a bulletproof car which was to collect old currency notes from a bank in King's Cross and take them to the Bank of England for destruction. Nevertheless, it went on relentlessly. The police had taken the position of the Jaguar as a central point, and from there made a circle approximately half a mile round it. This took in an enormous area of London, which included the mass of guest and boarding houses serving the University of London, huge apartment blocks, as well as hundreds of small, pleasant streets of Georgian or late Victorian houses.

By sheer chance, Janice Westerman's flat was easier to approach by car from the perimeter of the circle than the heart; it would be among the last to be visited, and the officers in charge of the search estimated that if they could keep fifty men on the job they would be finished by Friday at the earliest.

Most of the time, now, Janice was frightened, for she had no doubt that she was being kept prisoner. So far all their supplies had lasted, but they would have to contact some shop, or else cut down on eating, before this day, Wednesday, was out. She still did not know who her jailer was, but she knew that he was bordering on the pervert.

He would not put on the radio, and she had no television. The thing which saved her from absolute boredom and despair was the record player. And in some moods he would jump up from his chair, pull her from hers, and dance to frenzied music, wild, exhilarating, breathtaking. He would start to drag her clothes off, but before he had finished he would collapse, exhausted; too exhausted for love.

After these periods of fierce excitement, he would become moody. Wherever she was, whatever she was doing, he would stare at her. All this time, he kept on the wig, and she had no idea whether he realised that she knew that he wore one. It was after one of these unnerving moods, when he said: "Let's eat, I'm hungry," that she ventured, in the calmest voice she could summon: "We'll have to go to the shops, soon."

"We stay here," he said, sharply.

"But we must get some food," she protested. "We're out of milk and eggs, there's hardly any bread, most of the canned food—"

"We stay here," he repeated, and his expression changed, his lips tightened, there was viciousness in him.

She shot him a quick, nervous glance. "Unless you want to go hungry one of us must go and get something."

He said roughly: "If anyone goes, I go."

"But why can't we both go?"

"Because I say so."

Anger welled up in her, and had it not been for the accompanying fear, she would have shouted at him. *Freedom* was what she worshipped, was why she had left home, was why she lived here on her own, dependent on no one and beholden to no one – except, occasionally, her father. She liked the flat because the rest of the house was used as offices. She liked being on her own, without neighbours, without close friends, preferring strangers and short acquaintances; but this man—

"What's the matter with you?" he demanded.

"I want to do my own shopping," she said, "and I don't

see—"

He had sprung out of his chair, and was striking at her face, before she realised that he had moved. He struck her with the palm of his hand, a vicious blow on either cheek, and then drew back, breathing hard; his lips seemed to have disappeared into a thin line. Her cheeks stung and her anger rose to fury; but terror was greater. She sat and stared at him, wide eyed.

He backed away, saying viciously: "If you don't want me to get violent, just do what I tell you, in bed, out of bed, everywhere, all the time."

How could she take such an ultimatum from any man?

Whatever the consequences how could she possibly let him get away with it?

And if she did, this time, what hope was there for the future between them, be it a day or a week or a month. She had never been dominated and controlled and she wasn't going to be now. Whatever it cost her, she had to fight back. He was staring at her as these thoughts went through her mind and it was almost as if he could read the defiance in her.

Her heart was beating so fast she felt as if she were choking.

She couldn't get the words out, but – she had to. She could not meekly submit—

Unless she just pretended to, and at the first chance that came, escape. He couldn't keep watch on her all the time.

"Come on, let's know what you're thinking," he cried. He was in front of the chair, feet slightly apart, hands held out in front of him, the fingers curled and the palms downwards; an animal, about to pounce. An animal. A terrifying animal. But if she let him get away with this, where would her self-respect be? Her sense of independence?

"Get away from me," she said, "and I'll tell you."

"You tell me now."

"Get away from me, and I'll tell you," she repeated. "I don't want trouble with you, but I don't take orders from you or any man. So—"

He leapt at her. He grabbed her wrists as she tried to fend

him off, and hauled her up from the chair. It was as if he had a dozen arms and legs and fists and feet. He was breathing hard and she was gasping, quite sure that she was about to die. He dragged her into the bathroom and dumped her on a stool. She felt him yank her arms behind her and fumble at her wrists; he was binding her. At some stage he had fetched a rope she used when she went camping, and when her wrists were locked together with this he tied the other end to the lavatory chain that hung from the high cistern. When he had finished he was breathing in loud, animal gasps. He buried his fingers in her hair and pulled savagely, and then tied a scarf round her mouth and the back of her neck, so that she could hardly breathe.

She heard him go; heard the door shut; heard the key turn; and heard him move away. After that there was only the gurgling of the cistern and the harshness of her breathing. If she was to live, she had to breathe more gently, the gasps were almost choking her.

If she wanted to live—

The real question was, would he let her?

At the same moment, two bells rang on Gideon's desk, the internal one and the Yard operator's. He took a chance that the first would be Scott-Marie, lifted the other receiver and said to the operator: "Whoever it is, hold him or have him call back." He picked up the second receiver as he put the first down and announced: "Gideon."

"This is the Commissioner, Commander," Scott-Marie said, so formally that he must surely have someone else in the office with him. "I've decided that you must be guided by your own assessment of the evidence. Whatever decision you reach I will support, of course."

"Thank you, sir," Gideon said, not really sure whether to be pleased or sorry. "What time will you be free?"

"Not until late afternoon, if at all. But I shall be home this evening."

"Thank you," said Gideon, and rang off.

Scott-Marie had left him on his own and that was really how it should be, but he did not relish making the decision. Arrest as many as they could now, and warn the big shots; or wait and take a risk that even in a short time irreparable damage could be done. It wasn't often that the connection between police work and something as basic as cost of living and the life of the community was so obvious. For a few seconds he forgot the other call, but recollection came and he lifted the second receiver and asked: "Is my caller still waiting?"

"Yes, Commander." There was a click, and then Gideon heard Lemaitre's voice. "Hallo, George. We've found a store of Firex, some gelignite from a recently stolen store and a man who might or might not have died by accident. Shall I give you the story over the telephone, or come and see you?"

Before Gideon had answered, before he had really made up his mind what to say, there was a tap at the communicating door and Tiger looked in, apologetic and yet insistent.

"Sorry to worry you, sir," he said, "but Sir Bernard Dalyrymple is here – actually here, sir, waiting in the hall. May I tell him you'll see him?"

19

SIR BERNARD DALYRYMPLE

GIDEON said to Lemaitre: "Hold on, Lem," and to Tiger: "I'll gladly see him but won't be free for twenty minutes, possibly half-an-hour. Find out if he would like to do a Cook's tour of the Yard and if so get a senior man to take him round. If not, find him a comfortable chair and a cup of tea – what's the time?"

"Half past three, sir."

"Right." Gideon nodded dismissal and before the door had closed was on the telephone again to Lemaitre. In the way that he had acquired while in this office he had dealt with the two problems at once, and knew exactly what to say and do. "I need everything you can tell me now, Lem, and may need to see you later. Go ahead. "

Lemaitre, sensing his preoccupation and the need for urgency, brought him up to date with the Charlie Larsen, detonators and Firex situation, lucidly and yet vividly; and he managed to get a word in for Old Charlie Old.

"Is he still working?" Gideon asked, astonished.

"And still as blind as a bat in some things," replied Lemaitre. "We wouldn't have got this without him, but he's known Larsen for twenty years and didn't realise he was an explosives expert."

"I've known food thefts have been increasing for years but

didn't realise how big it was," Gideon replied. "Has the autopsy on Larsen been held?"

"No."

"Get it done, quick. This afternoon, without fail."

"Right."

"And we need to trace Larsen's movements for the past few days," said Gideon. "If he was the man who set fire to the warehouse we need to know very quickly, because he wouldn't do it for the excitement."

"Cash," Lemaitre said. "We found two hundred and fifty in notes stashed away, and some car or van keys. The only way we can check for that vehicle is to try all the cars and vans parked nearby. I've started the tracing, George, but—"

"There aren't any buts on this job, Lem."

"But I'll have to withdraw the chaps I lent for the house-to-house search for Dalby and that wench."

Gideon drew in a deep, almost painful breath. Lemaitre was quite right to raise the question, of course, and the decision had to be made. If they didn't find the escaped murderer and the girl soon, her chance of survival was slim indeed: but the other issue was so much bigger.

"Withdraw your men. I'll try to get some more in from the outer divisions," he added, but he knew that it was not going to be easy. August was still the great holiday month, policemen with families liked to be away in school holiday time, and forces were stretched thin. But he must try. He rang for Tiger, who appeared at once.

"Sir Bernard asked if he could see *Records* and the *Information Room*, sir. He's happy."

"I wish I were. Get onto all the perimeter – not the central divisions, and see if we can get some men in for the Dalby search. There's another emergency in NE and we're going to have to get some of their men back." He nodded dismissal and was lifting the telephone again while Tiger was still in the room, calling the superintendent in charge of the house-to-house search. The least he could do was tell the man what was to happen and promise as much help as possible tonight and tomorrow.

"Quite understand," the other said. "I did hope we'd be through by Friday but it could go into the weekend, now. Overtime pay all right?"

"Yes," replied Gideon.

"Someone will love us," the other replied, and rang off.

Janice heard the front door of the flat open; heard it close; heard "him" go into the kitchen. There were little thumping sounds, she could not place. She was beyond real thought and near coma, the ache at her arms and shoulders intolerable. She had swooned off several times and woken up to a sweat and a frenzy of fear.

The key of her prison turned; the door opened. Fear flared again, and merged with thought, and she wanted to plead with him, promise anything, if only he would let her go from this awful position.

He touched the top of her head; gently. *Gently.* He unfastened the scarf round her mouth and drew it away. He freed the rope from the chain and then from her wrists, and not once did he hurt her. He slid his arms round her waist and hoisted her slowly to her feet; she could not put any weight on them because her legs were so numbed; and pins and needles began an agonising tattoo. He eased her into the big room, and helped her onto her own bed. He took her wrists, one at a time, and rubbed quite gently.

"Okay," he said at last. "You just had to know who's boss, that's all. Do what you're told and you'll be all right." He smiled down at her as if he really meant that and was full of affection, then said: "I'll go and make a cuppa." Over his shoulder, he added: "I got some milk *and* cream, and – but wait until you see what I got. Enough for a week, I shouldn't wonder!"

A week?

A week here with him, now that she knew what he could be like?

She shivered violently . . .

And yet when he brought in the tea, put the tray on the foot of the bed, helped her to sit up and then poured out, the horror of her ordeal began to blur. He was obviously pleased with himself, proud of his shopping, ready for the time being to treat her well.

But what would happen if something she did or said sparked off another of those rages?

"Fascinating," declared Dalyrymple. "Absolutely fascinating. I'd read and heard a lot about the *Records* room and *Information* but to see them in action—" He gave a gentle smile and brushed his silky, near-white moustache with an affectionate gesture. He was a tall, willowy, pink-faced man; and his manner had the benignity of a clergyman who had absolute faith in his calling. But he was nervous, Gideon thought. "I'm most grateful for the time you're sparing, and dare to hope that it will be mutually helpful. Commander, am I right in thinking that you are more at home with a man of few words than one who tends to be over-prolix?"

Gideon smiled faintly, and said: "I like a man to be himself, sir."

Dalyrymple looked sceptical, and then he actually chuckled. "An excellent precept – though one not always wise to follow. And now to business. It has come to me through various trade sources that the police are deeply concerned with the matter of the theft of food in bulk. Further, that you have reached a fair and reasonable conclusion that stolen food finds a retail outlet, fairly quickly. Am I right?"

"Yes," Gideon said.

"And may I take it that what I say to you is in absolute confidence?"

"Unless it concerns a crime committed by you or known by you to have been committed, sir."

"You are precise, Commander. I have only suspicions; but I have held them for some time. It may be said that when one gets burned one looks for the cause of the fire. I am chairman of the Board and of the largest single food retailing business in the United Kingdom, and also this year's president of the National Association of Food Retailers." He paused to allow Gideon to take this in, and then added: "For my own company I am concerned: for many of the members of the association I am gravely perturbed. Many face ruin. My company faces severe reductions in reasonable profits and so reductions in dividends to our shareholders. We have known for some time – a year, at least – that a carefully considered campaign of price-cutting has drawn a great deal of our custom away. By our, please take it that I mean my company and the Association members. Price-cutting is not new. It comes in various guises – or should I say disguises? But now, for over a year we have faced genuine and steadily maintained price-cutting. As a result, many of our customers have gone to the place where they can get the best value." Again, he paused.

"So would most housewives," Gideon said, flatly.

"Yes, indeed. And most understandable." A smile appeared only to die at once. "We – our experts – have checked the prices against which we are having to compete. In the beginning we suspected, at this juncture we feel convinced that it, can *only* be done at a loss. There are no ways in which the price-cutter concerned can cut his own expenses – we have checked most carefully, have planted our own staff in a number of their stores and know that either they are losing money heavily in the short term to get the long term benefit—"

"How much do these losses run to?" asked Gideon.

"Our estimates are that one particular firm which has a variety of outlets, chiefly a supermarket chain, loses at least twenty-five million pounds a year." Now, the tall man's eyes were bright and questioning. *"At least,* Commander."

"A pretty high total for short term losses," Gideon said.

"Yes, indeed. Unless, of course, the losses are being offset by some other means." Sir Bernard Dalyrymple uttered these words both slowly and solemnly. Gideon studied him intently, wondering how much guile there was behind that benign exterior, sure there was a great deal. Dalyrymple accepted the long scrutiny without any sign of embarrassment and did not change his expression until Gideon said quietly: "Offset, for instance, by buying stolen goods in bulk."

"We understand each other perfectly," Dalyrymple said.

"I'm not sure I do comprehend the situation," replied Gideon. "If our estimates are right, the total thefts might be as high as five or as low as four per cent of the wholesale turnover. Would that make such a difference? Is five per cent sufficient for such serious price-cutting?"

Dalyrymple answered so quickly that he had obviously been prepared for the question. He leaned forward, and spoke with greater vehemence than before.

"Of itself, perhaps, no. But it is enough to attract a very large share of the customers. Its extra buying potential enables it to buy its other goods at higher discounts. Add these together – a profit from bulk thefts and a profit from extra large bulk buying, and – well, Commander: at least two sizeable chain stores are in difficulty, because they cannot match the low prices quoted by this particular company. They can give neither the quality nor the service competitively. And over two thousand small shopkeepers – food shopkeepers – have gone bankrupt in the past twelve months."

Gideon nodded, and for the first time since he had arrived Dalyrymple began to show some indications of what Gideon read as nervousness. Now he felt sure of this, for Dalyrymple went on apologetically: "This *is* only suspicion. The means, I mean. The facts are indisputable, but—well, the chain concerned has an American efficiency expert for its secretary, it *is* just conceivable that he has managed to cut corners honestly. Only just, but none the less conceivable. And it is also conceivable that some giant corporation overseas is trying to buy its way into our market at any price. But I know the American firms well, and—"

"You plump for the bulk thefts," Gideon said.

"I do," admitted Dalyrymple. "I've come to that conclusion since making the closest possible study of the present position and – let me freely admit it – since you have shown such an interest. It is a matter of great – delicacy. I can hardly accuse the Board of a successful competitor. And until I felt virtually certain I did not feel justified in coming to see you. Now—"

"Which is the company?" asked Gideon bluntly.

Dalyrymple drew in a deep breath, gave the impression that he would like to be evasive, and then answered unequivocally: "Quickturn Superstores, Commander. On their board is the Honourable Horatio Kilfoil, a son of one of the most highly respected men in commerce; Mr. Lancelot Black, who has been a member of our Association since he was a barrow-boy in London twenty years ago; one or two others who are – if I may say so—names simply to impress—the secretary is a Joseph Graaf."

Having delivered himself of these facts, Dalyrymple went on more easily. "May I beg you not to take action until you have evidence enough to satisfy you completely? I cannot offer evidence: only suspicions and indications. But if I am right, then this company is seriously attempting to control food in the United Kingdom. It is as easy to overcharge, once one has killed the effective competition, as to undercharge. And it might be disastrous to act too quickly, to catch the small fry and allow—"

Sir Bernard Dalyrymple stopped. Possibly that was because of Gideon's expression, possibly some warning signal sounded in his own mind. He shifted in his chair and then gave an impish smile.

"Now I am becoming prolix! And intruding into your province. Do please forgive me. And do please"—in a flash he was earnest again, even pleading, and his voice took on a deeper tone"—please prevent what could be a disaster, Mr. Gideon. Napoleon once called us a nation of shopkeepers and also remarked that an army marches on its stomach. A nation exists on its food; health, the Social Services, even political issues, depend on this." He pushed his chair back, stood up, looked down at Gideon and went on in a slightly lighter tone: "But you are fully aware of that, I am sure, Commander."

Gideon said: "Sir Bernard, I shall be sending some of my officers over tomorrow morning —Thursday —to scrutinise all the reports you've collated. Can I rely on you to give them every facility?"

"No one will ever be more welcome, and no one will have greater facilities," Dalyrymple promised.

"Could Sir Bernard Dalyrymple be trailing a red-herring?" wondered Gideon.

Could he possibly be the man behind it all?

He was still wondering when his Yard exchange telephone rang. He did not answer for a moment, he wanted time to think over Dalyrymple's visit, all he had said, all he had implied. He wished he had had the interview recorded, but there was still something distasteful about taping a conversation with a man who had come in good faith. The bell rang again on a longer burst, and Gideon lifted the receiver.

"Mr. Lemaitre, sir," the operator said, and almost on top of her words there came Lemaitre's voice with overtones of excitement.

"Commander? . . . We found the van for those keys. . . . It was parked in the yard of a Quickturn Supermarket in Whitechapel . . . . Got Charlie Larsen's prints all over it . . . . And what's more, it must have been outside the warehouse about the time of the fire. There are some of its tyreprints in a patch of oil, and the near-side front tyre of Larsen's van has a lot of oil in the tread. But that's not all—"

Lemaitre had to pause because he was out of breath; and Gideon needed the pause, to take in what he had been hearing. Thought of Dalyrymple had been driven from his mind, after mention of the yard of a Quickturn Supermarket. Between what Dalyrymple had told him and Lemaitre had to say, he had to make a decision: and he had to make it soon.

20

DECISION

"ARE you there, Commander?" Lemaitre asked at last. His voice was more controlled, the excitement less evident.

"Yes," Gideon said.

"Larsen's van was almost certainly used to carry at least twenty cans of jelly recently. There are some torn labels which came from the stolen cans, and marks on the inside of the van show where they stood. Larsen didn't keep his van very clean, he carried some kind of powder, probably flour, before, and it had settled on the floorboards. The tins made marks which match up exactly with the gelignite cans for size."

Gideon had a cold feeling in the pit of his stomach.

"Do you know where he took the stuff?"

"Can't even be sure he took it anywhere, there might have been another driver," replied Lemaitre. "But the answer's no, so far. I've put a general call out for anyone who's seen the van, it's a green Vauxhall with hinged sides and back."

"Send me a note of the number," Gideon said.

"Right."

"Lem—have you *any* idea what that gelignite is to be used for?"

"I know one bloody thing, it's going to be used to blow open safes, or strongrooms, or— hey, George!" Fresh excitement drove all formality away. "What about the refrigerator stores at Smithfield?"

"Do they lock them?" asked Gideon.

Lemaitre shook his head. "I don't know— Commander, I've an urgent message coming through. Will you hold on or shall I call you back?"

"I'll hold on," Gideon said.

It gave him time to think. He could do with it. *Now!* What did he really have? He answered himself without hesitation. He really had an explanation which would fit all the circumstances, and he had it from a man who was *the* authority on the subject. It was absurd seriously to suspect Dalyrymple, although he might reasonably wonder whether the man's concern was really for the general public or whether it was primarily for Serveright Stores. Nor did that greatly matter. Dalyrymple had tried to avoid implicating himself in a charge against Quickturn but he would not have named the chain, nor its directors, especially Kilfoil, unless he felt sure they were responsible. So, he came back to the question he had to decide: go slowly, amass more and more detailed evidence, *or,* make a move against the leaders, now.

He always favoured direct action.

But then, there was always a case for patience.

"Commander," Lemaitre said, without warning, "that was a false alarm. Sorry."

"Forget it," Gideon said, and rang off. He did not wait long before pressing for Tiger and sending for Cockerill and Firmani. It was time they were brought up to date. They would see things from a different angle.

Firmani arrived first, a spring-heeled jack even when he came into the office as sedately as he could. He had a folder of papers with him but hardly needed to refer to this as he made his report. There was as yet nothing absolutely positive, but the van salesmen all seemed to work for a small wholesaler who dealt in every variety of food, except fish. The company was an old-established one but had recently been taken over by a larger group of wholesalers.

"Who wouldn't be associated with Quickturn, would they?" asked Gideon.

Firmani made no attempt to conceal either his surprise or his disappointment.

"Connected is the word," he said. "The new owners are a subsidiary of Quickturn, who are extending fast in the wholesale *and* the supermarket sides of the business. What made you gue—er—how did you know?"

Gideon was saved the need of answering, for Cockerill came in at that moment. His face still showed signs of the battering it had taken, but there was a glint of satisfaction in his eyes. He said decisively: "I think we've got something, sir."

"Good. What?"

"We've been keeping tabs on six drivers and a few other men who seem to be involved," Cockerill said, "and they've nearly all had instructions to attend a meeting at Gnocchi warehouse tomorrow at twelve noon. Officially it's a union meeting, but the union knows nothing about it. They think the drivers might be planning a wildcat strike, but there's no certainty. We picked the information up at pubs, and—"

"Details can come later," interrupted Gideon. "You are quite sure of this?"

"They'll be at the meeting all right," Cockerill assured him. After a pause, he added: "We could get the place bugged – I mean wired up, sir – and find out what's going on. Safer than trying to get someone into the meeting, don't you think?"

"I'm bloody sure," declared Firmani.

Gideon said, slowly: "Yes, I suppose so." He pondered, but came up with nothing fresh, so he gave them the gist of what Dalrymple had told him. It was Cockerill who said: "A lot of things point to Quickturn, once you start thinking of them, sir. Most of these wholesalers do a fair amount of business with them."

"And the van salesmen . . ." Firmani explained to Cockerill, and then went on with a quick glance at Gideon: "It looks as if we want to wait for this meeting tomorrow, find out what's discussed, and then take action, sir."

Gideon looked at Cockerill.

"Is that how you see it?"

"I can't see it any other way," Cockerill admitted. "Would you like me to fix the mikes? It can be done after dark tonight. The roof is probably the best place, it's one of those with open steel girders, easy to fix. We don't have to break in."

After a long pause, Gideon said decisively: "Yes, fix it."

He telephoned Scott-Marie just before six o'clock, but the Commissioner was not yet back, so he wrote a succinct précis of what Dalrymple had said, and a message: "Am going to allow the meeting to take place, then visit Black and Kilfoil in person, early tomorrow afternoon. G.G." He sent this along to the Commissioner's office by messenger, and then called for his car, and drove home.

He had the uneasy feeling that he had missed something, but the uneasiness was dispelled at sight of Kate's radiant face when she opened the door to him. She gave and received a perfunctory kiss on either cheek, and then said: "There's a long letter from Penny! The tour's been extended by a month, *she's* turning out to be the star soloist – Alec put that in! – and they plan to get married as soon as they get back. And George – *look.*" There was a postscript at the end of a long, often barely decipherable letter, which read:

"*Alec and I have struck a bargain: mornings when I'm free I can come and practise in 'my' attic!*"

And there was a PPS:

"*I don't know why I haven't realised it before, but I do love him so!*"

Gideon's heart was lighter than it had been for days when he sat down with Kate for the evening meal.

But in the night worry came back to him, and he tossed restlessly.

Joseph Graaf was restless, too; but he slept on and off, gradually getting used to the idea of a mass murder, the only thing now that would keep them high and dry. One thing he knew; there was no flaw in Lancelot Black's reasoning. Dead men could not talk.

Night and day had become much the same to Janice Westerman, and it was half past two in the early hours when she went into the kitchen to get a meal. Her captor wanted bacon and eggs, so bacon and eggs it would be. She knew he had bought the groceries from a small shop in a side street, for most of the things were wrapped in newspaper. She was taking the outer wrapping off the bacon, after putting eggs, butter, canned food and cheese away, when a photograph caught her eye: her own photograph! Astounded, she smoothed out the paper and saw a picture of "him" torn so that she would hardly have recognised it but for the one next to it, without a wig. On that instant, she realised who he was, and spun round towards the door.

He sat there: staring at her. It was no use pretending she hadn't seen the photograph or that she hadn't been shocked, and her breathing became shallow and fast. He came in, picked up the newspaper and read what it said, and then added: "So now you're a celebrity."

She made herself say: "No—no wonder you're so sure of yourself, darling."

She did not know how she got the "darling" out but she did know that it was effective, for there was a slackening of the tension about his mouth. They ate at the tiny kitchen table and every now and again he made some light semi-facetious remark, watching her covertly. When they returned to the living-room, he locked the door and put the key in his trouser pocket.

She knew, then, that she had just one chance: to fool him

absolutely.

Presently she went into the bathroom and came back wearing a loose negligée. She stifled a yawn as she slid, affectionately, onto his knee. His hands began to caress her. She put her cheek against his, nibbled his ear, did all those things which she knew he enjoyed. It would only be a matter of time before he pushed her onto the bed.

Quite suddenly, he did this, flinging himself on top of her. For a few moments they played, her heart beating tumultuously for one reason, his for another. They kissed, wildly, exploratively, and as they did so she slid her hands down, down, and began to caress him. His kissing grew gentler, softer: for this he loved. Slowly, slowly, she moved, and then, suddenly, she struck.

He screamed.

She flung him off, and as he writhed she snatched up his trousers and dived into the righthand pocket for the key, found it, rushed to the door and pushed it with trembling hands, into the lock. Helpless, groaning, bent double, he could do nothing. She pulled the door open and went racing down the stairs, out into the street shouting hoarsely, wildly, for help.

A taxi-driver, passing stopped; his fare leaned forward in utter astonishment at this confrontation with a naked, screaming girl.

"D—D—Dalby," she gasped. "Dalby's at—at my flat. D—D—"

The passenger was out of the taxi now, taking off his jacket to cover her, while the taxi-driver used his two-way radio to tell his controller to send for the police. By then Janice was shivering violently, and her teeth were chattering; she hardly seemed to realise what had happened.

Because of his broken night, Gideon slept later than usual the next morning, and was wakened by the telephone bell. When it stopped, he thought, I've been dreaming, and then he heard Kate speaking, and opened his eyes to see her fully dressed and standing by the telephone.

"Yes, I was just going to call him. Who?" She listened for a moment as Gideon struggled up in bed, and then handed him the telephone.

"It's Mr. Sharples."

"Ah," said Gideon, and was wide awake on the instant. "Hallo. . . . What have you got for me?" As he listened a smile began to dawn on his unshaven face, and it broadened into a grin and then into a laugh. Sharples went on as if thoroughly enjoying the telling, until Gideon interrupted, saying: "Thank heavens for that. Obviously a girl of ideas. Have you told Westerman?"

"He's been over and collected her."

"Good." Gideon sprang out of bed, his tiredness forgotten.

It wasn't really late; but it was nine o'clock before he left for Scotland Yard, acutely aware of the meeting to take place in three hours' time.

21

EXPLOSION

GIDEON left his car for a driver to put away and went straight up to his office. The whole place was astir with ribald, masculine humour; the story of the way Janice Westerman had outwitted Arthur Dalby on everyone's tongue. The coarseness which came so often neither annoyed nor surprised Gideon.

There were more folders than usual, and all the new ones had a pencilled-in title or heading. Two were bank robberies and one, very ugly, the murder of a night-watchman at a London departmental store. Everything was in hand; he needed to check and to get the full stories from men from the divisions who were already handling the case. All of this took a lot of time and it was getting on for eleven before he turned to the cases already in hand.

He did not look at the report on Dalby; that could wait. He gave only a cursory glance at Firmani's report; that had become virtually a side issue although it could have caused a dozen deaths. He opened the fat report on the FOOD BUYING CASE as Tiger had for some reason called it, and found everything he had been told last night down in black and white, but only one new positive factor in a note signed by Cockerill.

Microphones which will pick up everything at the meeting

have been installed. We have a rendezvous safe from observation at the top of Serveright's, a hundred yards away.

Microphones.

Gelignite.

A meeting of a dozen suspected men, and if the police knew of a dozen then there might well be at least twice as many more; perhaps three times as many. Why? Instructions for thefts, hijacking, the transfer of goods, everything in this racket must surely be passed on carefully, by telephone or by word of mouth. Why a meeting? Why—

Something seemed to explode inside his head.

For a moment which might in fact have been seconds and might have been a minute or two, he felt numbed by it; aware but not convinced. It was as if the explosion had brought a great flash of understanding into his mind, but another part of that mind refused to believe that anyone could possibly plan to kill a group of men in cold blood.

Dead men told no tales.

"It can't be," he said, and pressed for Tiger, who came at once. "Get Mr. Cockerill here, quick," he ordered.

"He's not in, sir. He's gone to superintend the surveillance on the warehouse so as to make sure all of our chaps are well hidden before any of the others arrive. Mr. Firmani's gone there, too – and I believe Mr. Lemaitre was going to join them. Er—there's one thing you should know, sir."

Gideon, getting up from his desk with ponderous deliberation, barked: "What?"

"The Honourable Mr. Kilfoil is going to address the meeting at twelve sharp."

"Oh," Gideon said. "Is he." He still felt as if the noise and the flash from the explosion were whirling about in his head. "Is he. Have a car sent round – not mine, one with a radio." He stood by the desk as Tiger went out, and for once Hobbs' stand-in looked as if he could not understand Gideon's expression.

He dialled Scott-Marie's number, knowing that the Commissioner might not be in. But he was in.

"The Commissioner."

"Gideon," Gideon said. "I've added everything together, sir, and I think that the suspects plus a meeting at that warehouse plus a large quantity of gelignite plus the probable existence of detonators plus Firex in large or small quantities add up to one major explosion. I'm going over myself, sir. We've an observation post at Serveright's close by. I'll radio instructions to our people while I'm on the way."

There was hardly a pause before Scott-Marie said: "I shall meet you at the warehouse, George," and rang off before Gideon could make any protest.

It was not a time for protest. There was an hour and a quarter – no, ten minutes – before he would know for certain whether he was right. The warehouse could be raided, of course, and any explosives rendered harmless, but that would warn some of the men and the place would be closely watched by the other side. He rang for Tiger, who appeared at once, saying: "Your car's on the way, sir."

"Thanks. Call the RAOC and ask them if they can have a man at our warehouse rendezvous in half-an-hour. Let me know by radio." He turned to the passage door and opened it – and Merriman, one hand raised to knock, almost fell onto him. Never before had Gideon seen excitement shining in this man's eyes and burn on his cheeks. In his free hand he held what looked like a photograph.

"Sir! I couldn't get you on the phone, but sir – that van of Larsen's, the van which the jelly was in—*Look, sir!*" He thrust the photograph in front of Gideon's nose, and went on in a voice that was very nearly a shout: "Top left hand corner, we missed it before but I've just seen—"

"I'm on my way there," Gideon said. "You come with me." Merriman's mouth dropped wide open; and then sheer joy chased the excitement out of his eyes.

It was no more than twenty minutes to the Gnocchi warehouse in Smithfield, and Gideon sat in the back, Merriman by the driver; Gideon had not realised how huge the man's shoulders were. Within five minutes a message came: "Royal Army Ordnance Corps will be there, sir." Gideon grunted, and leaned forward. "Give me that thing, Inspector." Merriman handed him the telephone, and he went on: "My office please. . . . Hallo, Chief Inspector Tiger? . . . I want a close but not obvious watch kept on Mr. Lancelot Black, Mr. Joseph Graaf and all the senior staff of Quickturn Limited. None of them is to be allowed to leave the country." He waited for Tiger's "Yes, sir," and handed the instrument back to Merriman.

"You knew, sir, didn't you?" Merriman said, quietly.

"I guessed: you brought the proof," Gideon said.

He thought that Merriman went red about the neck, but soon put the man out of his mind and concentrated on the next hour. He knew exactly what he wanted to do, but was far from sure that he could do it all. He watched the stalls and the open store fronts in Long Acre, the litter of vegetables on the cobbles, here and there some fruit or flowers, and then they came to the sector which had been razed. On one edge, nearest him, was the tall, new Serveright building, and soon they turned in. No policemen were in sight, but inside the building there were several, as well as plainclothes men, whom he recognised. He went up to the top floor, which appeared to be taken over by the police. One or two of Serveright's security men were about, and a Captain in the RAOC was talking to Cockerill.

"My goodness," Gideon said. "You were quick."

"I was at the Tower, sir – not far. How can I help you?"

"Have you seen the stuff we're dealing with?" asked Gideon.

"Chief Inspector Cockerill told me the size of the cans and I've seen a label," answered the bomb disposal man. "I know the stuff all right." He turned towards a window which overlooked a wide expanse of demolished buildings. In the middle was a single brick building; it was difficult to judge the distance but it must be a hundred yards away at least.

"If that blows up, will it do any damage anywhere else? Here, for instance?"

The Captain pursed his lips, and then slowly shook his head.

"I can't see why it should, provided no one's roaming about."

"Good. Can you get over and check when the explosion's due?"

The Captain nodded, then turned and went off, wearing a long coat over his uniform. He was back in twenty minutes, to report: "Twelve thirty, on the dot."

"Good," said Gideon, as Scott-Marie entered the office, and he raised his voice for the other's benefit. "We'll keep it clear," he went on. "Thanks." He turned to Cockerill and Firmani. "I'm going to let the meeting start, so that we get everyone who turns up," he said, "and at five past twelve, raid and empty it. We'll have about twenty-five minutes, so we want plenty of vans and Black Marias. *And* plenty of rush," he added, gruffly. "Then I want all the men we pick up, including Mr. Kilfoil if he's there, to see the place go up. If that won't open every mouth among them, nothing will." He looked about him at men who seemed stunned into silence, and then went on: "I'd like to arrest Mr. Kilfoil myself."

Scott-Marie came across and shook hands, then settled down to watch from the window.

They watched the drivers and others heading for the Gnocchi warehouse, many driving up in cars, a few walking. They saw a Rolls-Royce, undoubtedly Kilfoil's, draw up, and the member of the board of Quickturn get out of his car. That was a signal for the police to move in. No one inside the building had any indication of what was going to happen when the doors opened and the raid began. Kilfoil, standing on a roughly-made platform, began to complain, and Gideon said: "Wait twenty minutes, sir, and you'll see what it's all about."

They waited and watched with agonising tension, until suddenly there was a great flash; a roar; and fire. Debris went high into the air but none came as far as the forecourt of the building and no harm was done except to the morale of the men who had been told to go to the building. The only man who did not speak was Kilfoil. As Gideon charged him with conspiracy to defraud, he looked as if he would never recover from the shock.

An hour later, Cockerill, Firmani and Merriman entered the offices of Quickturn, taking the chairman and the secretary completely by surprise. They did not speak when charged with attempted murder and conspiracy to defraud. Within an hour, police accountants had taken over completely, within two, Dalyrymple's Association was working on plans to keep the stores open, until the legal and illegal aspects were sorted out. The two arrested men were taken to West London Police Court, and would be charged before a magistrate next morning.

Gideon managed to avoid most of the clamouring Press, and to get home reasonably early. There was a message from Scott-Marie, which said very simply: "The more I think about it the warmer my congratulations." Gideon put the message in a box in which he stored his few mementos, watched the television news, rejoiced with Kate and felt both deeply satisfied and a little flat at the same time. He was tired. The pace of the past week told on him. He would be glad when Hobbs was back—

But Hobbs and Penny would want a honeymoon!

Suddenly, he thought: Or are they having one now?

He thought of the changes in society, conventions, morals and beliefs, and he wondered how Janice Westerman would face the future.

"Daddy," she said to her father, a few days later, "I can't, I just can't, stay here. I don't know where I'll go or what I'll do, but I'll be all right. I'm one of the wild ones – but I can look after myself."

"Janice," her father said with a wry smile, "I really believe you can."

JOHN CREASEY

GIDEON'S DAY

Gideon's day is a busy one. He balances family commitments with solving a series of seemingly unrelated crimes from which a plot nonetheless evolves and a mystery is solved.

One of the most senior officers within Scotland Yard, George Gideon's crime solving abilities are in the finest traditions of London's world famous police headquarters. His analytical brain and sense of fairness is respected by colleagues and villains alike.

'The finest of all Scotland Yard series' – New York Times.

GIDEON'S FIRE

Commander George Gideon of Scotland Yard has to deal successively with news of a mass murderer, a depraved maniac, and the deaths of a family in an arson attack on an old building south of the river. This leaves little time for the crisis developing at home ....

'Gideon of Scotland Yard emerges as one of the most real working detectives in modern fiction.... A sympathetic and believable professional policeman.' - New York Times

John Creasey

The Creepers

"The prisoner's hand was thin and bony ... And in the centre of the palm was a pinkish mark. It was the shape of a wolf's head, mouth open, fangs showing. Although it was what he had expected to see, Inspector West felt a twinge of repugnance a stab not unrelated to fear. It was the fifth time he had seen the mark of the wolf – the mark of Lobo."

A gang of cat burglars led by Lobo cause mayhem as they terrorize the city. They must be stopped, but with little in the way of evidence the police are baffled. Just how can Inspector West manage to do this in what is a race against time before more victims succumb?

"Here is an excellent novel of law enforcement officers, harried, discouraged and desperately fatigued, moving inexorably ahead under the pressure of knowledge that they must succeed to save human lives." - Cleveland Plain-Dealer

"Furiously exciting" - Chicago Tribune

"The action is fast, continuous and exciting" - San Francisco News

JOHN CREASEY

THE HOUSE OF THE BEARS

Standing alone in the bleak Yorkshire Moors is Sir Rufus Marne's 'House of the Bears'. Dr. Palfrey is asked to journey there to examine an invalid - who has now disappeared. Moreover, Marne's daughter lies terribly injured after a fall from the minstrel's gallery which Dr. Palfrey discovers was no accident. He sets out to investigate and the results surprise even him . . . .

"'Palfrey' and his boys deserve to take their places among the immortals." - Western Mail

INTRODUCING THE TOFF

Whilst returning home from a cricket match at his father's country home, the Honourable Richard Rollison - alias The Toff - comes across an accident which proves to be a mystery. As he delves deeper into the matter with his usual perseverance and thoroughness , murder and suspense form the backdrop to a fast moving and exciting adventure.

'The Toff has been promoted to a place of honour among amateur detectives.' – The Times Literary Supplement

15292618R00099

Printed in Great Britain
by Amazon